Edie on the Warpath

EDIE ON
THE WARPATH

+-+-+-+ ❁ +-+-+-+

E. C. SPYKMAN

Harcourt, Brace & World, Inc., New York

TO BARB

✦ Contents ✦

✦ *Edie on the Warpath* ✦

One

•┼• ❀ •┼•

RIGHTS FOR EDIE

What to do with Edith Cares for the winter of 1913, when she was eleven years old, was causing the John Cares family of Summerton, Massachusetts, more trouble than she would probably ever be worth. At least this was the opinion of her brother Theodore, who gave it freely when he came home on weekends from college.

"And if you keep on clicking your jaw at people when you chew," he added at Sunday lunch after the roast beef had been served, "even a reform school won't take you."

The reason Edie could not stay at home this winter was because Madam, her stepmother, had begun to have attacks of asthma and would have to go to Florida for her bronchial tubes. Madam's children, The Fair Christine and Lou, who were not very old, only six and four, could go with her because they had Hood, their nurse, to take care of them. Edie's other brother, Hubert, was in the sixth form at his boarding school, so he was all right, and Jane, her older sister, had become a social butterfly who was supposed to lure men into taking her to football

games, dances, and balls. "Quite a job at that," as Hubert
remarked—especially when she was meant to take care of
Father in the time left over. Therefore, there was no one
who could pay attention to Edie.

Usually, any Cares who had needed more time and attention and more education at the age of eleven had been
sent to their grandfather's in Charlottesville after he had
moved to town for the winter and had lived in his third
floor room with gas jets and black cupboards, roller-skat-
ing every day to a good Charlottesville school. This time
Grandfather had drawn the line at Edie. He was too old
now for that sort of thing, he had told Father.

"Well, what sort of thing?" Edie asked, clicking her jaw
at Theodore because he kept his eyes on her.

She was not particularly anxious herself to go to Grandfather's. She drew the line at him, too. Whenever they
played Old Maid together and he won, he looked at her
through the bottom of his spectacles as if it meant something, and whenever she won and looked at him, he sat
back in his chair and said: "But I can't be, I've been mar-
ried already." Was that fair?

So she did not mind not going to Grandfather's. What
she did mind was being shunted around like an old railroad car that no one wanted to see coming down the
track, so she would really like to know what sort of thing
kept everyone going on and on about her, the way they
did about the Suffragettes or President Wilson.

Even if they had been willing to listen, Edie would not
have considered telling them why she particularly wanted
to stay at home this winter. In the first place, she herself
approved of her own school, Miss Lincoln's. All the Cares
children had been to her and knew about her parrot and

how she baked cookies three times a week. For herself, something extra had been added, Edie knew—outside crusts of fresh bread with butter and honey at recess. "For an exceptionally *good* child." So how did they like that!

In the second place, Susan Stoningham, her best friend, had come to live just up the road, or, if you went across lots, only as far as two fields, a swamp, and a lawn away.

In the third, fourth, fifth, and all the other places, Edie liked the new house they were living in. Father had built it. Nobody had wanted to leave the Red House in the valley where they had all been born and grew up. Even Edie herself had lived there for nine years. But Father had thought that being on the highest hill in Summerton would be good for Madam's breathing, so the Red House had vanished and there was the Lawn House instead. Edie liked it. Everybody liked it. It had big rooms, big halls, big corridors. Madam had done them in green and white and gold, and her own parlor was rose, as Mother's had been in the Red House. Even Theodore thought this was tactful. They all had rooms of their own, and the boys had the whole top floor away from everybody.

"And that's the *most* tactful," Edie said to Hubert one day as they were walking down the hall to the library. He did not get mad but only tripped her up and left her on the floor.

From Edie's own room—indeed from any room in the house if you looked out the right window—you could see almost the whole of the west end of Summerton; the meadows that made up the family dairy farms, the chain of Reservoir basins that took water to Charlottesville, the woods that were on top of the small hills, and the scattered valley trees—giant oaks and elms and maples that

the cows stood under—and the masses of corn steeped in
the sun and baking. That had been this summer. The sun
and wind had seemed to be everywhere in this house, so
that it smelled of flowers, hay, and, now in September,
corn. She wanted to be in it when it smelled of snow. If
there should be an ice storm, she would be able to see
every branch and twig for miles. She even looked forward
to mud. There was a foot scraper between two horseshoes
fastened to the stone outside the front door. It had never
been used yet. She meant to christen it the first time she
broke through the swamp ice on her way back from Susan's. Hobbling back from the stables (which Father had
put quite a way from the house to keep the house air
pure), with a stone in her jodhpur boots, she kept stopping to breathe in the late afternoon air. It had been a
marvelous ride. She and Susan had cantered up and down,
around and around the soft clay roads of Aunt Charlotte's
demesne. On the way home, while the horses were cool-
ing, they had chanted their chant.

"I love Summerton.

"I love the trees.

"I love the grass.

"I love the dirt.

"I love the water.

"I love the stones.

"I love the woodchucks.

"I love the snakes.

"I love the mosquitoes."

In Susan's opinion, you couldn't go further than that,
because mosquito bites swelled her up.

There would be three horses for them to ride this winter when the others weren't home. There would be

Widgy, her small brown dog to take to the Reservoir looking for muskrats. There would be Susan's rabbits—well,
they weren't much, but they had little rabbits that got to
look like marshmallows. There would be football games at
Hubert's school—that was in Summerton because it had
been started by Mother's father—and it was, very conveniently, not far from the Lawn House. You could see a
hundred boys in a single afternoon. There would be—
Heavens, of course she could not leave home. She had
forgotten the most important thing of all. Susan, whose
father was a minister, was teaching her religion. When
Grandfather was in Summerton, Edie went to church with
him every Sunday. She had fallen in love with Greg Robinson, the boy who carried the cross at church, and was
doing her best to persuade God to make him look at her—
just once.

With this sort of private life going on, Edie could not
see how anyone could expect her to leave Summerton.
They did, though. Aunt Charlotte had asked Father if he
wished his daughter to grow up a hottentot, and when he
had to say "no," she said she would be back when she had
thought things over.

"And heaven knows," Hubert had said, "what dark plot
she may be hatching."

The other relations, who belonged to Mother, attacked
Madam on the sly. They called her on the telephone
about Edie's riding pants and her hair—particularly her
hair. Edie did not think her hair was bad; it was thick and
yellow and went with her blue eyes, but she had chopped
it off last summer with the carving knife, and to keep it
out of her eyes, she pushed it back behind her ears. It
made her look, they said, like a young tiger cat.

"Not bad at that," said Hubert, when he heard it.

It had been a pleasure to snarl at him, and it was a pleasure to keep arguing with everybody.

"I just want to stay here. Why can't I?"

"If you say that again, I'll—"

"I'll say it till I'm dead. Why can't I? Why can't I?"

"All right," said Theodore. "Look—do you really want to know?"

"Yes!"

"All right, I'll tell you," said Theodore, bracing his hands on the table so that he lifted himself a little. "You are *nothing but a girl* and have to be taken care of. You're the weaker sex, and all you'll ever be able to do is your knitting. Why don't you get that into your silly noodle so we can have some peace?"

Edie would not have known there was to be a parade of suffragettes in Canboro, the little town just beyond the west end of Summerton, if Father had not mentioned it. She knew that there were suffragettes because he fumed whenever he read the tiniest bit of news about them, but he found the parade a sort of extra and said things out loud about suffragettes. Taking off his glasses and laying them carefully at the side of his plate at supper the next Sunday night, he told Jane and Edie that to lower themselves to act like anthropoids would be to send the world to perdition.

"What's an anthropoid?" said Edie.

"Go look in the glass, little one," said Hubert, under his breath.

Father's advice was that if she wished to see an anthropoid, she had only to look at the Sunday paper.

After supper, she and Jane rushed to get the rotogravure section of the *Charlottesville Herald*. Jane brought it out and spread it on the big hall table. Edie and Hubert crowded her shoulders.

"I suppose that's what he's talking about," said Jane.

Half the front page was covered with pictures of the parade that had just been held in Charlottesville. As far as Edie could see, they were just a lot of women in big hats walking along carrying flags and banners. She couldn't see much difference in the way they looked and the way Madam and Mrs. Stoningham did when they were all dressed up. But Jane's finger stopped at one caption.

"Some of the ladies wore masculine attire," she read.

"Where?" said Hubert. "Hey, let me look! You mean *that?*"

One woman was having an argument with a policeman. She had on a pair of bloomers. The picture made Hubert put his hand over his mouth and rock around the hall bent double. He came and looked again.

"What's she got on, a pair of balloons?"

"Skirts *are* awful," said Jane.

"But not that," said Hubert, rocking around again. "Even you and Edie can look better than *that.*"

It was nearly half past eight, and he could not stay any longer. He had to get back to his school by nine or be docked his next weekend, but he had time to take the paper away from Jane, tear out the part with the suffragettes, fold it carefully, and put it in his pocket.

"My reputation will be *made*," he said.

Jane and Edie did not know quite what to say to each other when they were left alone. All Edie knew was that the parade in Canboro was going to be on the day of the

Canboro Harvest Festival, and she was now sure that the
suffragettes meant to spoil all the other fun. She had been
looking forward to the Harvest Festival. All the family
went to the Canboro Festival every year. They were quite
famous there. Hubert had once managed to capture the
greased pig by stumbling on top of him, Father had won a
prize for a pumpkin over all the relations and outlying
farmers, Theodore had won jumping prizes on his mare,
and Edie herself last year had been given a silver dollar
for hitting the head stuck through the canvas three times
running-with a baseball. She had collected quite a crowd.
She had heard a man say to a friend:

"Sure, she should have a ball team of her own."

She wanted to try again this year and had been practicing her baseball arm with Fatty McHenry down the road.
Now maybe it would all be spoiled.

"What do those old suffragettes think they're doing?"
she asked Jane. "The police ought to get after them better."

"Oh, no!" said Jane. "They just think women are as good
as men, that's all, and want to be allowed to vote."

"What's the good of that?"

Jane kicked the table leg a little as she bent over what
was left of the paper between her outstretched arms.

"Well, I suppose if you could vote, you could make
laws. You might even get to be President."

"Oh," said Edie.

Although it was a marvelous night with a full harvest
moon, she did not go out. She did not want to look at
anything outside. Instead she went to her room and sat
cross-legged in the middle of the floor with her head
hanging down and her eyes closed. Her mind floated in

darkness until it began to see some things. If she could become President, she could put all the men in traps. She would get bear traps, with teeth. She would keep them there until they stopped talking. She would starve them until they couldn't talk. Accidentally she opened her eyes and saw her room and the carpet and became sensible. No president would ever be allowed to do such things. Not even President Woodrow Wilson. Father had said, "Thank God, there are limits," and bear traps would probably be one of them. She dropped into a hole of despond. Even if you died and went to heaven, the angels all had to wear skirts. She hit her head on the floor. There was no way out and no help, no help, no help. She straightened. The suffragettes thought there was. They must or they wouldn't be making a fight for it. Edie's head lifted and so did her heart. After half an hour she had to find Jane. As she might have known, Jane was in her own room scribbling in her old diary. Edie stood at the door and made a small noise until she was heard.

"I'm a suffragette myself," said Edie.

Jane's voice came after her when she was part way down the hall. "That's fine, but I don't know what you can do about it."

This was just the kind of thing about which Jane could be wrong. If Edie had a good idea, she did something about it. She had had ideas before and had done something about them. A lot of the time what happened was pretty good. If those suffragettes were to vote for her for President after a while, she had better get started helping them right away. She wondered if Susan could be persuaded to come to the parade. No, she wouldn't ask her. She didn't think Susan would see the point about the suffragettes. She wanted God to do everything. Well, she herself would appreciate any help God might condescend to give her, but it was a very good chance to find out if He was willing to do anything for girls as well as boys. So who could she get?

Edie could not think of anyone to be a suffragette with her until one morning when she was taking Widgy to the Reservoir to look for muskrats and they were walking past the McHenrys' just above the dam. There was no one around, but just seeing the house did the trick. Why not Fatty McHenry? Edie and her family had lived just opposite the McHenrys' when they lived in the Red House. Boney McHenry was Jane's friend, and Fatty was hers. They had done every kind of thing together. If she went to the parade in her French boy's fishing suit that Madam had brought her from abroad last summer—just to show those suffragettes they didn't need to dress in balloons— why couldn't Fatty go in her clothes so there would be two of them? They could dress in the Lawn House store-room down the cellar, get out by the cellar stairs, and get off to Canboro on their bikes just by telling Madam beforehand that this was the way they meant to go and that they would meet the family at the Festival. Edie thought this plan so good that she stopped on her way back and made Fatty come out and talk to her.

"It's not the best *I* ever heard of," said Fatty when she had explained.

"Why not?"

"For one thing, you're thinner than me."

"You can wear a sash and a jacket that'll hide what's extra," said Edie.

He gave in finally, and told Edie so, because he had

been to see Julian Eltinge, The Great Female Impersonator, at Loew's Orpheum in Charlottesville and had not been impressed. There wasn't much to it, he said, if you had the right kind of clothes and a hat or two.

"You can have my *best* clothes," said Edie, "and I've got a hat that'll come right down to your ears."

In spite of this, Fatty was gloomy and uncertain. He wanted to prove he could do it, but this seemed almost too rash a way.

"Look," she said, "we can take your pants in the bike basket, and you can change as soon as the parade's over. I thought you said, 'Anybody could do it.' I suppose that was just boasting."

It was, and Edie knew it all right, but it made Fatty put up or shut up. He said he would do it. Edie did not mind if he was a little discontented. He had been discontented a lot of times about her arrangements, and then they had had a wonderful time. But he had to keep on arguing.

"How am I to know which outhouse to use to change my clothes?" he said as she got up from the grass, just as if he were trying to get out of it again.

Edie pretended not to hear him. She wasn't going to talk about outhouses with Fatty McHenry. It wasn't a respectable subject, and anyway, she was not going to let him get started again with objections.

"You'll be perfectly all right," she said. "You're just supposed to be *one more woman*."

This did not seem to make him much braver, and she had to admit, as she watched his feet scuffing up the lawn as she went off, that she felt a little discouraged. She could see that Julian Eltinge's influence had become quite weak. Maybe he wouldn't come.

Fatty did come, however, on the Saturday morning of the Festival, and Edie got him safely down the cellar. She had been, she thought, marvelously efficient. She had planned for him to come after the family—Madam, Father, Chris, and Lou—had driven off in the Packard. She had smuggled her dress and petticoats down to the storeroom without being caught by Cook or Gander, the maid. She had even sneaked two horse blanket pins out of the harness room in case the waistbands would not meet on Fatty in the back. She turned on the storeroom light, showed him everything, and then modestly left him while she went up to her room and put on the French boy's fishing suit. She apologized to Widgy and shut him in the bathroom, opened the door to the back hall and listened for Gander, and then scuttled down, expecting to see Fatty all ready. He was not all ready. He had not shown the least sense about being a Female Impersonator. Her piqué dress was on wrong side to because he thought the buttons came in front, and her petticoats sagged before and behind. He was standing in front of Edie's shoes, looking as if he did not have much hope about anything.

"They won't go on," he said.

And the petticoats would not stay up because he was as big in front as at the sides.

"Why didn't you use the pins?" said Edie.

She had to do it for him. He said he did not know how to use horse blanket pins on himself. She could see he had tried, because he had pricked his finger and the petticoats were all over red polka dots.

"Never mind that," said Edie. "They won't show."

She gathered all the sagging petticoats together and

tacked them to his shirt, and then with a good deal of
tugging and twisting, she turned the piqué dress around
and Fatty began to look like something she had seen before. It was not a girl exactly. Maybe it was the Widow
O'Warty in Mrs. Wesselhoff's books. But she was not going to tell him, and anyway, the sash put around twice to
hold in his stomach was a great improvement, and the red
jacket was really good. The more you put on Fatty, she
could see, the better he looked. This was most noticeable
when he put on her hat and could hardly be seen at all.
But there was one thing that made her stare. How could
he in a couple of seconds, just by putting on a dress and a
hat, have begun to grow a mustache? Edie quickly turned
down the brim of the hat. It was lucky there was no mirror downstairs. But even the danger of this was forgotten
in getting him into her shoes. No cramming would do it.

"You must have bunions," said Edie. "Can't you shove a
little harder?"

Fatty sat down obstinately on an old box. "I'm not going to have my feet killing me the whole afternoon," he
said.

Edie managed to solve it. She flew upstairs and came
back with Jane's nice new white sneakers.

"That's more like it," said Fatty, "but they're going to
flap a little."

The main thing was that he was willing to put them
on.

"How do I look?" he said, standing up when he was
ready and turning himself around.

"Almost like Julian Eltinge," said Edie, "if you could
pull your stomach in a little."

Fatty tried but gave it up. "I can't hold my breath all day. There are plenty of fat girls. You see 'em everywhere."

"How do *I* look?" said Edie.

Admiration was forced out of Fatty.

"Gee, you're it, even if you do look scalped with your hair under that cap. Come on, let's get going."

His eagerness lessened at the top of the cellar steps. He hugged the jacket around him. "These things are drafty, aren't they?" he said.

"I have to wear them all the time," said Edie. "Did you ever think of *that?*"

But Fatty kept on thinking of nothing but himself. He wanted to ride his own bicycle, not Edie's.

"You can't throw your legs around like that if you're a girl," Edie said. "It shows your underclothes. Just put your foot through the middle and press the pedal." After wobbling along a few yards, he was pulled off by letting the end of his sash get caught in the gear chain. He made an awful fuss, saying he had knocked his teeth out.

"You're not even bloody," said Edie.

But she had to whip into the Lawn House front door, find a towel in the downstairs toilet room, and bring it out to clean him up with.

"I bet my lip's swelling up," he said, not even grateful.

"Never *mind,*" said Edie. "If we don't get started, we'll miss the parade."

Going down the Lawn House hill, he couldn't keep his skirts in order, and the wind blew his hat over his eyes. They were only at Uncle Charles's gateway when he said his legs were raw from the bike saddle.

"Pedal standing up for a while," said Edie. "I do, often. But anyway, *hurry up*." She could never have believed that a man could have so much the matter with him.

And it was nothing—nothing—compared to his having to pick a fight the minute they got to the main street of Canboro. At the corner, without a car or a cart in sight, he got off and said he felt weak.

"Weak!" said Edie, getting off, too, and peering under his hat. "You look healthier than I ever saw you before in my life. You're bright red, and your sweat's coming out like anything."

Fatty said he was not a horse, so his sweat didn't mean a thing. He felt weak just the same. He went ahead, wheeling his bike, but he went very slowly and weakly. He was not going to tell Edie, but his exhaustion was being caused by a thought. Some of the people in the cars and carriages that had passed them on the road had spoken to them. One man in a buggy had slowed down and taken a good hard look. "Yer little sister looks kinder tuckered, don't she?" he had said to Edie. Fatty could not get over the fact that he had been taken absolutely for a girl. He had begun to wonder if he really looked like one. He had meant to, of course, but now he was finding it alarming. In spite of all Edie could do, he finally stopped at a patch of front yard where a boy with a ball was playing with a dog.

"Come *on*," said Edie. "I tell you we'll miss it."

Fatty only stood with his feet apart, stuck.

Then he had the nerve to say to the boy: "Hey, let me throw it once, will you?"

The boy gave him a look and paid no attention. He bounced the ball for the dog again.

"Hey," said Fatty, "don't be a dog in the manger. Let me try."

He cupped his hands.

The boy still did not answer, stared for a second, and then threw the ball to Edie. "Give it to her," he said tolerantly. "I don't suppose she can send it far."

Edie caught the ball all right, but Fatty had it out of her hands before she could close her fingers.

"I'll show you how far I can send it," he said. "Do you want to see your old ball again?"

He leaned way back, stretched out his arm behind him, and sent the ball high in the air. It was all right, Edie saw; it flew up to the top of the house and came down on the lawn, where it bounced to deadness. The only thing bad about it was a tearing sound she heard on Fatty.

"Thanks," said the boy, watching the ball, but he did not go to pick it up. He looked at Fatty instead. "I could have you arrested," he said, "so my advice is, you'd better vamoose."

Fatty walked away with what Edie knew he thought was great dignity, but she was behind him and she could see what had made the tearing noise. Below the back of the piqué dress there was a drooping frill of white.

"Fatty, stop!" she said.

"No!"

"Yes!" said Edie. "You have to. You're coming apart."

Fatty took one look over his shoulder and then down the block. There were people coming. He went over to the edge of the sidewalk and sat down with his feet in the gutter and his back to the passers-by.

"Here I stay," he said glumly.

Edie would have willingly left him there forever if she had not felt she must get him to the parade.

"Look," she said. "Stand up a sec, slowly. I'll put my foot on it. Then we'll shove it down the drain."

They waited until the people on the sidewalk were well past. "Now!" said Edie. She planted both feet firmly on the frill as Fatty rose. There was a more frightful sound of tearing than before, and part of the petticoat dragged in the gutter. Only part. The horse blanket pins were too good. Fatty sat down again.

"You didn't do a very good job," he said. "Try it again. Holy cats, there's a policeman coming."

By the time Edie saw the policeman, he was standing right over them. Fatty crouched together like a bird. Let Edie who was respectably dressed take care of it.

"Are you having a little trouble with the young lady?" asked the policeman.

"Or," said the policeman more severely after he had caught sight of the petticoat, "was it your intention to undress in the public streets?"

How could you possibly explain to a policeman that Fatty was just what Father called "a chump" who thought he could be a Female Impersonator and got upset at the slightest thing. Edie still did not answer.

"If so," said the policeman, "I'm here to prevent it. Get her up, me lad. The best thing'd be you'd come along with me. We're having enough trouble with females today."

"Where to?" said Edie.

"The station, in course," said the policeman.

Edie might have gone. Any Cares knew what happened if you "resisted the law." But it was too much for Fatty. He was not going to a police station in a girl's clothes,

particularly not in her underclothes. He bounded up so
hard and fast that the policeman had to step back. It gave
Fatty time to get started, and Edie was not going to desert
him. They went down the Canboro main street as fast as
Fatty was able to run entrapped by embroidery. When
the policeman shouted after them, Edie stooped, picked
up the petticoat ruffles, and drove Fatty on this loose rein,
furiously. They pelted almost without knowing it right
into the middle of the suffragettes. The parade hadn't
started, and the women were milling around outside the
Canboro Town Hall. Fatty dived into them.

"Saved," he said. "We're saved, Edie. Has anybody got
a pair of scissors?" he asked a circle of women.

"As a matter of fact, *I* have," said a woman with a ban-
ner. "Here, child, let me trim you up. You've had a little
accident, haven't you? That's what comes of petticoats,
you see."

"I do see," said Fatty, while he turned as the woman
trimmed. "That's why I'm at this parade. My name's
Cares."

"And who is this?" asked the woman, looking at Edie.

"That's my sister," said Fatty. "She thought you ought
to be shown how to dress."

"Hm, yes," said the woman. "Very nice. But pants are
unladylike, you know. We are all being careful not to do
anything unladylike."

A very bossy woman came striding through the crowd
shouting: "Form up, form up by fours." When she came to
Fatty, who was now trimmed and as decent as he ever
would be as a suffragette, she said: "What's this child
doing here?" Another woman made a face at her and
whispered.

"A Cares child? From Summerton?" the bossy woman said. "Whole family much against us. Quite a feather in our caps. Give her a flag and let her walk in front.

"Would you like to lead the parade?" she asked Fatty. He nodded with his head bent down. "Shy little thing, evidently. What's your first name, dear? What? Edie? Didn't know there was a Cares that size. So peculiar looking, too. But we must make the most of you," she went on to Fatty. "Come, get between these ladies. You better take her hands if she's shy. What did you say, dear? Your sister's here? Where?" She turned on Edie and looked her up and down. "What *have you got on?*" she said. "No, I don't think you better march. We can't risk ridicule. Join the crowd if you like, but don't join us. We're doing everything to be ladylike."

The suffragettes were getting into line, and Edie's attempts after this to get into line with them were met by elbows and hips that rushed past. Fatty was being taken off under her eyes, protected by a whole mass of women and using her name to make himself one of them. She tried again to join the ranks. This time a tall pretty woman slowed up and leaned down to her. "We are anxious not to do anything to debase our womanhood," she said very earnestly. Then she was swept along. Edie began to doubt their good sense. They didn't even know what to do so they wouldn't be laughed at. She was so occupied thinking about them that she had no feeling for what might be behind her. Without the least warning an enormous hand was put on her shoulder.

"Not so fast, me lad," said the policeman.

"You let go of me," said Edie, twisting. She walked backwards as fast as she could.

"You're under arrest," he said, coming forward.

"Why am I?" said Edie. "I haven't done anything."

"None of your lip, now. Just come with me and I'll do you no harm."

This, Edie did not believe. She had "resisted the law," and she was still resisting it. If she were caught, she would be in another trap. She kept backing and the policeman kept on coming as much as the crowd would let them. Then the crowd, getting interested, opened up a path. It was now or never. She would have to run for it again. Just as his hand came out to get her, she ducked and turned, saw the open lane in front of her, and knew she could go down it faster than that gigantic cop. She certainly could have, but in turning she brushed against a stomach and nearly lost her cap, her precious cap. She made a snatch for it as she felt it going, got it in her hand, and started to really run. Her yellow hair tumbled around her ears.

"Ah," said the crowd.

It wasn't sympathy. As soon as it had breathed, it closed up. There was no way out to freedom. The cop had her. Edie faced him while he came toward her, taking his time. He was so big that he had to squat to look at her with what she thought was the ugliest red face she had ever seen.

"Sure, 'tis only a girl," he said.

Those awful, terrible words. They must be pasted on her. This time she'd get 'em off. She drew back her clenched fist and, as Theodore afterwards expressed it, "slugged him one."

Although she did hit him and there was a nice mark on his cheek a little purpler than the rest, it wasn't much of a slug against all that fat face, as Edie herself could feel, but dodging, he lost his balance and sat down hard. The crowd roared. They were skunks, but they roared, and if she had to die right there, she didn't mind.

Still, it was this, she knew, that made Officer Clancy so mad that he lugged her off to the police station, where, sitting on a hard bench that hurt the back of her knees, she almost wished she *had* died. She was questioned by another officer at a desk—her name, her age, her address, and Father's name and whereabouts.

After a hundred years there was a trampling at one of the doors, and a whole bunch of suffragettes were pushed through by a whole bunch of policemen propelling them on with their billies. At the back of them was a dwarf who was trying to walk on the sides of her feet. Crickets and grasshoppers! It was Fatty! They had caught him, too, and he looked more like the Widow O'Warty than ever. He had lost her best hat, and her piqué dress had some- how gotten worked up into pleats over his stomach. If she had been a policeman, *she'd* have arrested him. Back of him was Father. He was not being propelled, but for a dreadful second Edie wondered if he had been caught, too, perhaps on her account, and was going to have to go to jail with her. It was suddenly the most frightening thing of all. What would she do with Father in a cell! He would be no good at taming rats, and if there were bugs, he wouldn't be able to stand it at all.

To her great relief, Father left the suffragettes freely and came over to where she was standing. She stood up in order to meet her doom, but what Father said was: "Sorry, old girl, they had a hard time finding me." He put his arm around her shoulders and looked down at her.

Edie's smile was uncertain. Why should a suffragette-hater like Father be saying things like that?

"You seem to have gotten yourself into a peck of trouble," Father said, giving her shoulder a pat, "but it's a relief to me to see you haven't joined up with those misguided women like your running mate there."

Fatty tried to pull down his dress under Father's eye.

"He went in my place," Edie said quickly. "They wouldn't let me."

"The more chump he," said Father. He didn't seem to really understand, but his name was called and he had to go to the desk to see what he could do for them. Edie sat down beside Fatty.

"Gee, it was great," Fatty said at once. "Glad you made me do it, Edie. The old hens were furious when I took off my hat."

"If you didn't make such silly remarks," said Edie, "I'd think you were a regular Sidney Carton."

"Gee," said Fatty again. His stomach got bigger because of the compliment, and he had to tug the dress down again. "Well, don't give yourself away. *My* family don't care."

Then Father came back with their sentences.

"Fatty, you're clear," he said. "You've only been a thumping idiot. Edith, you will have to apologize to the Sergeant for your behavior to Policeman Clancy."

"No!" said Edie.

"Yes!" said Father.

Edie got up slowly and went to the desk. She put her hands behind her back, looked up at the Sergeant, and waited. The Sergeant looked at her and waited. It was certainly a good thing that Father was separated from them by some suffragettes, so that he could not hear what they said to each other, because it was nothing. The Sergeant began to rub his chin.

"Miss Cares," he began finally.

"I'm not," said Edie. "I'm Edith." She didn't think she ought to pretend to be anyone important.

The Sergeant cleared his throat. "Whoever you are," he said, "you should know that Officer Clancy is one of the most respected men on the force. He is liked throughout Canboro, and especially for his kindness to children and animals."

"Well, so am I," said Edie.

"Furthermore," said the Sergeant, raising his voice, "'tis an offense to be striking police officers."

"I only hit one," said Edie, "and he's bigger than me."

For a moment the Sergeant seemed distracted. He was looking at something behind her, so she turned and looked, too. It was Officer Clancy, who had come in and was talking to Father. He was about twice as broad as Father, and it made quite a funny sight, but the Sergeant did not seem to think so. He frowned across the room.

"Here, Clancy," he said, booming, "this is your prisoner. Get your apology yourself."

Officer Clancy waved it all aside with his hand.

"Ah, let the kid go," he said. "We was both in a bit of a temper. Let her father here handle her case. He's been telling me what he'll be doing to her. So, it is right, sir?" he said to Mr. Cares.

"Yes," said Father. "Yes, indeed. That's all then? I want to thank you gentlemen for your fine Irish courtesy." He shook hands with each of them. "We can go," he said, coming back to Edie and Fatty, "by the kind permission

of these officers." Father waved his hand around the room.
They got up, but Father hesitated, holding his chin. "To
my lasting regret," he said, "the top of the car is down,
and the newspapers are waiting for those misguided
women. Well, come on, we'll have to weather it. Keep
your heads down and keep your mouths shut."

Father's good advice did no good. Harold McHenry,
the Female Impersonator, and Edith Cares, the suffragette, who had struck a policeman, were in the Sunday
rotogravure.

"If it hadn't been for that," Theodore told Hubert, "I
daresay the old man would have let her off."

But there it was for all to see. The newspapermen
thought it was smart to be so funny. It made Father real-
ize what had happened, and Edie was not let off. Her
French boy's fishing suit was taken away for what he
called "an indefinite period."

"But that didn't do anything," Edie said.

"It apparently caused you to break the law," said Father. "Come now. Whatever made you do such foolish
things?"

Although a lovely warmth rushed up from her stomach
to her throat because his voice was nice and he had been
nice, Edie kept her mouth shut as she had been told to do.
Even to get the fishing suit back she would not open it.
Madam tried and Jane tried to find out her ideas and her
reasons, but she would not explain. Hubert was the only
one who could finally get her to speak. If he had been
"made" at school by the first suffragette pictures, he was
"unmade" by the last ones, and he had to have an answer,
he said, as to what great scheme of life led her to indulge

in the practice of hitting cops. If he knew this, he said, he could hit the people *he* needed to for getting fresh.

"My womanhood," said Edie. "I did it for my womanhood."

Hubert, lying on the lawn before Sunday dinner, clasped his hands on his head and rolled back and forth as if he had a pain.

"How can anyone make any sense out of that?" he said.

"You could if you were me," said Edie.

Two

✦ ❁ ✦

THE GOOD SAMARITANS

It was Sunday again when Aunt Charlotte with her two guardian Pekingese, Wong and Mr. Wu, came to reveal her great thoughts about what was to be done with Edie. She almost always came on Sundays. It was to be sure and find Father at home, Madam said. Everyone else considered it inconvenient. Sunday dinner was the time when The Fair Christine and Lou could come down for dessert, and depend upon it, as Theodore remarked, they could always arrange to make trouble. This time it was because of Lou's ice cream spoon. Every time she put it in her mouth, she brought it out again still loaded with ice cream. No one could stop her. Theodore tried by pinching her tactfully under the table, Jane made faces, and Hubert showed his tongue with a large white lump on it.

"That's about the way it looks," he said.

Lou kept right on doing it, with her eyes turning to each one of them in turn.

It lasted until Lou took a long happy breath and choked. Ice cream went everywhere, but mostly on Aunt

Charlotte. Lou had to be removed by Father's command and showed she did not think it was fair by holding onto anything within reach, her chair, the tablecloth, and finally Hubert's hair.

"Not much of an omen for *you*," said Hubert out of the corner of his mouth to Edie as they left the table.

It made her go and get Widgy out of the coat closet. She had put him in there on account of the Chinese dragons, but if this was going to be that conference about her, she was sure she needed protection as much as Aunt Charlotte. In the library she held him in her lap with one strong brown hand. He behaved perfectly. He kept crawling to the edge of her knees to have a look at the dragons and toss his head at them, that was all. They did not give him a glance. They took up their positions at Aunt Charlotte's feet with their tongues half hanging out of their mouths and waited for someone to attack her. She took up a position herself in a big straight chair with her skirts spread out and considered Edie.

"The child certainly needs attention," she said.

Luckily Madam was upstairs with her asthma.

"It wouldn't hurt her to be exposed to a few manners and a little culture," Aunt Charlotte said. "I will take her myself, if she can be properly clothed."

"Will she go?" said Jane quickly. It seemed to her a frightful exile, and she meant to do what she could for Edie. Edie said nothing. She might be thinking it over. Perhaps manners and culture in a house that smelled like Aunt Charlotte's appealed to her. She had not tried it before.

"What about Widge, though?" Edie said, crossing her legs on the firestool to make a good nest for him.

Aunt Charlotte took an even longer look at Widgy but did not answer.

"You have your dogs; why can't I have mine?"

"We will not discuss it," said Aunt Charlotte. "I simply make your parents the offer. I cannot have Wong and Mr. Wu exposed to the habits of mongrels."

"Why not?" said Edie. "Anyway, he's *not* a mongrel."

Aunt Charlotte rose and shook out her skirts. "When you have made up your mind, you can let me know," she said to Father. "I believe something could be done with the child."

After she had gone, more time was spent in trying to make Edie see reason about going to Aunt Charlotte's than Theodore and Hubert could, in their wildest dreams, have imagined possible. Jane said, for instance, that she would take care of Widgy.

"You!" said Edie.

Everyone knew that Jane couldn't be trusted to remember a thing.

All right then, Edie was coming home Friday night till Sunday afternoon, wasn't she? Widgy couldn't starve in that time with all the things he managed to get out of Cook, and she had the whole weekend to solace him for being abandoned. Father thought of that. He also thought she should go to a good school and learn something.

"You might like it for a change," said Hubert.

"You might learn to spell," said Theodore temptingly.

"You might be able to make friends with Wong and Mr. Wu," said Jane.

Madam thought she should remember that Aunt Charlotte's house was always full of flowers and that the circus came to Charlottesville.

Finally Edie got up.

"All right," she said. "I'll go, but I would like to make just one remark. You are taking away my mother—my stepmother, I mean—my home, my pony, my farms, my only friend—I don't mind so much about my brothers and sister—and now you want to take away my dog. Is that fair?"

After this one remark she walked out of the room with Widgy at her heels.

Right then Theodore and Hubert knew that this was the end of the argument. Although here was a heaven-sent opportunity to get rid of the kid and get her educated, their stepmother naturally turned out to be as weak as water.

"Whatever she said to the Old Man," said Theodore while he was shaving upstairs and Hubert was sitting on the edge of the bathtub, "the poor orphan child is not going to be put out of her home. Phui!" he said, blowing soap all over the mirror.

Edie's opinion of her stepmother was very different from Theodore's. She thought her the brightest, wisest, bravest woman in the world. Was there anybody else, even Father, who would have taken her side against Aunt Charlotte? Would anybody else even have known that they ought to stand up for her when she herself had almost consented to going to prison? She was wonderful and even super-wonderful. Edie wished she could do something for her like letting her know in time that the house was on fire or saving her from drowning, but the only thing that Madam ever really seemed to want done was errands, and Edie had been forbidden to touch the

Ford. She did think of one thing. Instead of praying for herself about Greg Robinson, she prayed that Madam would get over her asthma. It didn't work. In fact, as the cold weather began coming, so did Madam's asthma, worse and worse. Edie complained about this to Susan.

"I don't know what you can do about God," Susan said. "He doesn't seem to want to listen to you. But if you want to thank your stepmother, my mother says to pass good deeds along. You might try being a Good Samaritan."

"And pick up people in the street?" said Edie. "I'm not strong enough. Anyway, there aren't any nowadays."

"There are horses, though," said Susan.

"Are you sure they count?" asked Edie. Susan was so stuck on animals that she could be awfully unreliable.

Whether they did or not, and just as if prayers were somewhat answered, she was able to pass on her step-mother's good deed to a horse within two days. Whatever arranged it, Hood got one of her sick headaches, which meant that all she could do was lie in bed and moan. Gander was willing to feed and dress The Littles, as The Fair Christine and Lou were sometimes called, but she couldn't be "skirting the length and breadth of the town" as well, and Pat, the coachman, couldn't be found, so Edie was asked to go to the drugstore and get a prescription from Mr. Shrewsbury. She couldn't do it without Susan. How could she? It was a mile there and a mile back, and at any moment she might meet Greg Robinson going down for a soda, so they agreed to meet at the Congrega-tional Church.

It was a short errand, and as they had not seen each other since last night, they prolonged it with a milk shake. Then, Mr. Shrewsbury out of the kindness of his heart, offered them another. Feeling wonderfully well after this and with the prescription in Edie's pocket, they started back. They had not met Greg Robinson, but what they did meet was a crowd outside McCarthy's saloon. Something was happening in the middle of it that they couldn't see, so they ran up the bank on the opposite side of the road.

"Oh, oh, oh," said Susan, "I can't look. A poor old horse has fallen down. I think he's dying."

She sat down and wouldn't get up.

"It's our *chance*," said Edie.

She crossed the road and, by wriggling and pushing, got through the grown-up legs. Susan was right. An old skin-and-bones horse had just lain down in the dust of the road and looked as if he meant to die. Someone had loosened the traces, and an old skin-and-bones buggy stood behind him. Edie knew all about them. They belonged to the Hermit who lived in the woods behind the Main Dairy farm. He came to town once a month, and everyone said every time that, from the look of him and his horse, he would never make it again. But they had kept on coming, until now the horse had given up. He wasn't dead yet, though. You could see his ribs move a little. He might be just taking a rest. Or he might need some food and water. He looked exactly like Widgy that time he spent ten days in one of Miss Lydia Hardy's woodchuck holes. Why didn't somebody try to help him? The men were all standing around just looking.

All of a sudden Edie remembered where Pat was and why Madam had not been able to find him. It was the week and day he took Father's chestnut gelding to the blacksmith shop. The blacksmith shop was just around the corner from the drugstore. She wriggled back through the grown-up legs and ran.

Hallelujah! Pat was there, sitting on the old tree stump the blacksmith used for a chair.

"What's got you now, Miss Edith?" he said as she dashed at him.

"The Hermit's horse," she said, panting, "has fallen down in the road by McCarthy's, and no one knows what to do. I thought you could do it."

But she was not at all sure, after all, that an old man with glasses could get a fallen horse up.

"Well, now, let us see."

Pat took off the glasses, folded them, and put them carefully in his breast pocket.

"Hurry," said Edie. "Oh, hurry!"

"I doubt he'll be dying yet awhile," he said as they went up the little hill to McCarthy's.

"Out of the way, me lads," Pat said as he went through the crowd.

Edie told the whole story to Madam when she at last got home with the prescription. How she had found Pat, how some men had brought bottles from McCarthy's saloon. "But I brought the water," she said. How Pat got the horse on his feet, shaking and trembling. "And Susan and I brought him home," she said. "We did it very carefully and slowly, one on each side. He's in the barn now, and we're going to cure him."

Madam was sitting in her own room in a chair holding onto its arms. Her face was very thin and her eyes very big, and she was trying hard to take proper breaths.

"The Hermit," she said, "the horse belongs to him, Edie."

"Pat talked to him," Edie said. "*I* talked to him, too. He minded at first, but not any more. Pat's taking him home in the Ford as soon as he gets back from the blacksmith shop. He can have the horse as soon as he's better."

Her stepmother's big eyes still looked as if she might be doing the wrong thing.

"We did it for you," Edie said quickly. "We just did it for you because you let me stay at home. We passed it along."

It was so embarrassing that she had to turn and get out of the room.

The next day both Madam and the horse were better, so much better that they could both walk around slowly and easily, and Edie arranged for them to meet. Madam came halfway down the drive and the horse came halfway up.

"Well, he did need care, darling," Madam said.

That evening Edie was sent for after supper. Her stepmother had not come down, but then she often did not nowadays if her asthma was bad. It had not become worse. In fact, she said it had all loosened up, and she would be almost well tomorrow, but she was staying in bed to have a rest. Edie leaned against the bedpost. "You look wonderful," she said. Madam did, all covered with tiny pink satin bows from her bedjacket. She was not only good, she was beautiful, Edie thought. Why couldn't she get well? Why couldn't *she* do something to make her get well?

"Father said I was to come up," she said to her stepmother.

What Madam wanted to see her about was Hood. Hood was all tired out taking care of the children.

"She is?" said Edie. "What does she do?"

Anyway, that was what probably gave Hood the sick headaches, and before she started for Florida, Madam wanted to give Hood a vacation. Edie nodded. It was probably a good idea. But there was more to it than that. Madam herself was going away for a week to a hospital to have some tests taken, to see if they could find out about the asthma. That was an awfully good idea. But what about the children?

"I find it's impossible to get anyone to come to Summerton for such a short time," Madam said. "Jane has promised to take care of them mornings and evenings, but that leaves the daytimes."

"How about Gander?" Edie asked. She was pleased that her stepmother was asking her advice, but honestly she didn't know who could take care of Chris and Lou—especially Lou. She sat down on the end of the bed to discuss it. Gander, her stepmother said, had enough to do already.

"How about Edith Cares, the Good Samaritan?" her stepmother said.

"ME!" said Edie, getting up off the bed.

The idea was so much too much for her that she found she had to go away as fast as she could. She wanted to smile from ear to ear and had to keep her mouth tight closed in order to stop it. She nodded at her stepmother, then sidled out the door and walked very fast to her own room, where she locked the door and crawled under the bed. Madam had not only given her something to do for her; she had also given her the most important job in the Lawn House—taking care of her own children! Madam thought she could do it, and she knew she *could* do it. She had often and often watched Hood bringing them up as badly as possible; wiping their hands all the time, watching their faces for the least signs of hot and cold, telling them "don't," dragging them back. She had often and often pitied their boring lives. They would have to do a little work, of course, in order to earn some excitement— Father had made them all learn to work, and why he hadn't with The Littles everyone had wondered—but that could be exciting, too. They could learn a little Good Samaritanism themselves perhaps. She would return them to Hood so well trained that perhaps even Hood would give in and change her ways. She would have liked to begin on the spot and, in fact, went to look for her charges, but Jane had taken them off in the Ford, so she went to see Hood instead. Her room was still dark, and she still had a bandage over her eyes.

"Hood," Edie said from the door, "I'm going to take care of Chris and Lou for you."

"Heaven help us!" said Hood. "Go away, Miss. I can't stand anything more. Go away."

The aspirin, Edie was afraid, had not done any good, but still, it was just like Hood to be discouraging, and it was just like her to make a fuss on Saturday morning when she was going away. She had to give a thousand advices to Chris and Lou; she had to straighten their dresses and give them pats and finally kisses and a thousand "Be goods" and a million "Don't bother your mothers" and ONE last awful look at Edie, saying: "And you attend to your business, Miss Edith, and don't be letting your little sisters come to harm."

If she had really meant any of it, Edie considered, Hood should not have given in to teasing at the last minute and let the children drive down with her to the station. It was no way to keep them from harm. What Edie knew was going to happen did happen. When Hood got out, so did Chris and Lou, as quick as puppies, and like puppies you could not put them back in. They followed Hood in to get her ticket, and out again with Mr. Hurlbut to get her baggage checked, and back again to the outside bench, where they sat huddled against her as close as they could get. Pat had to wait, soothing and talking to Harry Houdini, Father's carriage horse. Pat did not like it; he said the morning would be flown from him, but in her important position, Edie did not have to mind him. She was going to follow her own ideas. When she heard the train whistle, she turned and walked directly to the bench.

"Now, Miss," said Hood. "Let me go, children. I must get on the train."

"No!" said Lou loudly. "I don't want you to."

"We don't want you to, we don't want you to," Chris began singing. They pranced and danced around Hood up to the train steps.

It was lucky that the brakeman was there. Somehow he got hold of part of Hood and hoisted her up the steps.

"Good-by, darlings, good-by, good-by," she called. "I better disappear, Miss," she said to Edie.

Edie caught hold of whatever she could grab and held the children back.

"Chris," she said, "if you walk down the platform, you can see her through the window." Chris went. But not Lou. Oh, no. Lou wriggled like an eel, got her hand free, and made for the train, just as the engine gave the cars a tremendous jolt. There was nothing to do but get her and hold on, no matter what happened. As she separated Lou's hands from the hand rail, Lou sat down. Edie sat down with her, her fingers around Lou's wrists like handcuffs. People who wanted to get on the train had to step around and over them and had to listen to Lou yelling with all her might. One lady stopped. "I had a nephew like that," she said. "He went into convulsions." Lou was throwing herself around as if she had a convulsion already. Well, let her have it. Anyway, she wouldn't be under the train. Suddenly from behind her someone leaned over and just as suddenly Lou disappeared. Edie let go and looked up. It was a man. He had Lou under one arm and was carrying her just like a pig to the carriage with her kicking feet stuck out behind. He tossed her onto the front seat, where Pat put one of his great hands on her. Edie turned and shrieked for Chris and then ran for the carriage. She had to thank him. That wonderful man! Where was he? Where did he go to? She couldn't find him.

"Pat, what happened to that man?"

Pat hadn't noticed. He was keeping Harry Houdini in order with his left hand and Lou in order with his right. So Edie never did find him. She had not seen his face, only his back and his gray suit. He might be anybody. In all her life she'd never get over not being able to thank him. He had been just like God, or if God couldn't possibly be paying attention to Lou, he had sent an archangel.

"I didn't thank him," she said to Pat. "I didn't have a chance to thank him."

But Pat was not at all interested. He leaned across her and Lou and gave Chris a hand up and then gave Lou another look as he started Harry with a slight lift of his hand.

"The little one has blood on her, Miss. Did she have a fall?"

Edie's heart nearly jumped out of her. "Where?" she said.

"On her mouth then," said Pat. "Take a look. Has she cut herself?"

Lou was sitting as quiet as a mouse and tasting her lips, but when Edie wiped them, there was no cut, not even a bruise.

"Maybe she's knocked her teeth out," said Chris. "Open your mouth, you."

Lou opened obediently. The teeth were all there. But so was some of the blood. It was on the handkerchief Pat had supplied. Perhaps she was bleeding inside from her convulsion. Pat made Harry hump along a little faster, but he seemed the slowest old horse in the world.

"Anyway," said Chris as they were passing the Episcopal Church, "she's a cannibal if she likes her own blood."

Lou wriggled. "I am not a cannibal," she said.

Chris kept looking at her as if she did not believe it.

"You get away from looking at me," said Lou. "I bited 'at man; 'at's why I've got blood on my mouf."

"You're the most terrible girl in the world," said Chris fiercely. "You ought to be thrown away."

Edie was glad to have someone say it. She was thinking exactly the same thing about someone who would bite an archangel. But Lou paid no attention. She sucked her lips all the way up the Main Street so that they could all hear her. At the beginning of the Lawn House drive she looked up at Edie.

"'At man had good-tasting blood," she said.

Just because things had started out a little wrong, Edie

was not going to be discouraged. Anyone could see that Hood had spoiled the children and had kept on doing it right up to the last minute. Now that her bad influence was gone, they would see that no one was going to pamper them and would get used to being ordinary people instead of princesses.

What caused real discouragement, Edie found, was Gander's interfering. She met them at the front door and pulled them all inside as fast as she could shove, quacking, "Be quick, now," because she thought it was going to rain. And just as if God were obeying her, it began, not in a drizzle, but in great big heavy drops.

"A little rain never hurt anybody," Edie said, resisting the shoves.

"Play some games with them, surely," said Gander. "Indeed, the poor mites would be naturally lonely the first day."

"If you would just mind your business," said Edie.

That only started some more quacking.

The only game Chris wanted to play was Lotto, but there were two things the matter with that. Lou was too young, and the counters had been used for mud-pie decorations long since. Well, they could use beans, Chris thought, and Lou could just sit around.

It worked for a little while. Lou got under the hall sofa and had a good time sucking her thumb. When a bean dropped off a Lotto card, she reached out a hand under the ruffle and drew it in like a raccoon. "Let her," said Chris. "It'll keep her busy."

"Well, don't you eat 'em," said Edie to the raccoon, "or you'll have a bean vine growing out of your *mouf*."

She thought Lotto was a terribly dull game. She would

instead have liked to take them out and show them some
good mud puddles to stamp in. The rain was coming
down harder and harder, and there would be bigger and
bigger puddles. Maybe it would rain all week, maybe forever.

"We could run to the stables," she said.

"Hood wouldn't like it. We never go out in the rain. It's
wet," said Chris.

How, thought Edie, could you teach them anything,
sitting all day playing Lotto with a lot of rolling beans?

It was desperation at last that made her plan to escape
and risk pneumonia. When Gander went to take her afternoon's rest, Edie dressed The Littles hurriedly in their
rain things, telling Chris to shush and shush and shush,
and made them race her to the stables. The rain on her
own face felt like cool, delicious animal paws, but Chris
said it was going down her neck and Lou said it was going
down the whole of her. "I can feel it in my toeth," she
said.

On the way back she tried to make them enjoy life a
little by pushing them against the dripping shrubs, and
she took them all the way to the Reservoir dam to see the
sight of the pouring tons of water. They both shivered at
it and said they were cold. She would not let them go
home though, not yet.

She tramped them to Grandfather's because it was Saturday and she knew he would be at home and in. In order
to let them enjoy life, she allowed them to get down on
their hands and knees at the front door and race into the
sitting room behind the chairs so that they could give
Grandfather a surprise.

"BOOM," they said together as they rounded the first chair.

"Take care! Take care!" Grandfather called.

Of course, it had to be the day he had decided to fight flies. He did it every September by putting fly paper all over his sitting room floor, with just a narrow path between for him to walk through, and of course Chris and Lou were in it before they could stop themselves and stuck all over with fly paper and flies. Grandfather laughed till the ash fell off his cigar and all over his trousers, but that didn't stop him. He kept on saying, "Ho-ho," while they struggled and writhed and collected more fly paper whatever they did. Nellie Flaherty had to be summoned and Mary Bright. They were commanded to peel Chris and Lou, but a lot of good it did. They were still sticky from head to foot, and they were dotted and plastered with flies.

"Ho-ho-ho," Grandfather kept on saying until he finally thought of the rain. "Get them out in it," he said, pointing with his cigar, "and mind you hurry them home."

He was still ho-ho-ing with his head back as Edie got them out of the front door. "You're going to have to walk home without your coats and hats, see," she said, "and we'll go by Uncle Warren's brook and you can get into that, and we'll cross Aunt Charlotte's meadow and you can rub yourselves off on that, and you can walk through the little hemlocks at the top of the hill and rub on those, see." And it was still pelting with rain.

They did it all, weeping and furious, and it did some good, but they had to be soaked in the bathtub, too, and a good many flies had to be picked off one by one. Naturally

Gander came and looked and said that if they hadn't gotten their deaths, it was only by the Lord's mercy; but the Lord's mercy for Edie was that when they were ready for supper, stringy and waterlogged, Jane was waiting and said she would dry what was left of them. She seemed to think the fly paper was funny, too.

When she woke up the next morning and saw that it was still raining, Edie wondered how she could give *herself* pneumonia and just go back to sleep again. But even if she could, she couldn't. Her stepmother would never understand how anyone could get tired of taking care of her children on the very first day. Besides, their training had only just begun. She really *needed* more time to get them into shape. No horse that she had ever heard of could run the first day after he was taken off grass. Feeling better, she was dressed by the time Jane came in.

"Lou has an earache," Jane said.

Edie sat down hard on her bed. "Is it pneumonia?"

"I don't think so, but I'm telephoning the doctor. You'll have to see him when he comes. I'm going to Charlottesville for the day, and Father is going to the hospital to see Madam."

The doctor was new because their old Doctor Harris had died, and as far as Edie could remember, no Cares had ever had him before. Nobody knew him, not even Gander or Cook. Edie felt as if Jane must have invented him. But he came. He couldn't see much wrong with Lou —certainly not pneumonia, no—though mastoiditis might set in later.

"What is that thing?" said Edie.

"Bone decay," said the doctor.

"How do I know if it sets in?"

"The child will be in pain," said the doctor, and went out of the door with his black bag as if he had fixed everything.

He had certainly fixed Edie. To have bones decay in your head was about the worst thing she could think of, and as far as she could see, the child was in pain right then.

"It hurts, it hurts, it hurts," said Lou when Edie dashed upstairs to see.

The only one who could stop her was Chris, who visited her and whispered in her good ear. But Lou would not stop for long. She shook her head from side to side during the whispering and then began again. She said it all day long, and by the time Jane got home, and then Father, she was saying it with little screams in between.

Edie told Father about decaying bones.

"Call that fool doctor again," Father said.

But it was Sunday. The fool doctor dared to tell Father that "the child was hysterical" and to wait until morning. Father came up himself to see. Lou buried her face in the pillow and would not look at or speak to him. Chris kept standing first on one leg and then the other and saying: "She isn't being naughty, truly she isn't, not now."

"How do you know so much about it, Miss?" said Father suspiciously.

But Chris would not tell.

In the morning Lou's crying was like a tin whistle. She did not say anything any more; she just screeched thinly and steadily. Jane had kept on spraying her ear all night long as the doctor had recommended, but it had not helped at all. Lou would not drink or eat or do anything but hold her ear and make that sound. She would not listen to Chris whispering or even open her eyes. It was bone decay for sure, Edie thought, and Lou would probably die. She wondered if Lou's whole head would go at once or slowly and dreadfully get soft and melt.

"Don't *you* be such a goat," said Jane, "as well as everybody else. Anyway Father's taking her to the Canboro Hospital right after breakfast."

But before they could start, the fool doctor came with his black bag and asked how the patient was this morning. In spite of everyone's hating him, he seemed to think he had a right to go upstairs, and they all followed him as meekly as if he were Solomon.

This time he did not spray Lou's ear. Instead, he felt all around it with his fingers, pressing behind and in front. He sat down on the bed, leaned over, and pressed a little harder, while she tried to get away. He caught her ear.

"Hold still, young lady," he said.

Suddenly Lou's ear gave a pop, and something jumped out of it and onto the floor. Chris went after it like lightning, picked it up, and held it out.

"It's a bean," she said. "She wanted to have a bean vine grow out of her ear."

It was only half a bean, though, and the doctor had to get the other half out with his instrument. He did not say anything, Father did not say anything, Jane did not say anything, and nobody knew where or how to look, except Chris, who patted Lou on the head and said: "You'll be all right now, you foolish girl."

It was certainly a terrible job to harden up such tenderfeet as Chris and Lou, but Tuesday was bright and warm and glorious, and Edie could start again. She decided to introduce them to the heifers that roamed around the meadow below the Main Dairy. Heifers never hurt anybody, and when you made friends with them, you could pat their noses. Any kids would like that. It was a mystery that Chris and Lou did not. The minute the bunched heifers sniffed and shuffled their feet, Chris and Lou turned and fled, which made the heifers move off after them. Edie nearly had to kill herself running to get in front of the heifers and shout them off. They all braked at once and turned away shamefaced, but Chris and Lou thought themselves dead at least. All Edie could think of to soothe them was to take them to Nurse's store in the village and let them guzzle ice cream and fudge marshmallow, the most frightful breaking of training that anyone could imagine.

It was Pat who had an idea for Thursday. Standing with his hands on his hips, inspecting The Littles, " 'Tis a shame," he said, "the two of them aren't horseflesh."

It only took about half an hour to turn them into it. Pat helped make the rope bridles and reins and let them use a clean box stall with shavings to be shut up in. Edie drove them as a pair, a prancing, head-tossing, and cavorting high-stepping pair of park hacks, gave them broken-up crackers for oats, and let them drink out of the real watering trough. They were turned out to graze in the small paddock behind the stables, though this was rather disappointing. They would not throw up their heels and race around as they should and have some fun. Lou stood and gnawed the fence bar, and Chris sat languidly on a post. They both kept saying: "When can we get out of here?"

"Horses can't talk," said Edie.

"We can," said Chris.

She had to bring them in, but she had had time to find a

currycomb, and she hitched them up on the barn floor and ran it over them hissing properly.

Pat saw them docilely pacing around the stable yard.

"Well now, Miss," he said, "you turned the trick, didn't you?" Edie gave him a small, modest smile. Maybe he was talking too soon. But she got it to last till five o'clock, and when they suddenly became girls again and said they wouldn't play any more, she was proud of them. They would make two nice park hacks with just a little more training.

Friday morning while Edie was having one more piece of toast to get up her strength for the day, Chris found a dead bird on the terrace, and all the rest of the week disappeared. There were no beans, no heifers, no marshmallow fudge, no park hacks, nothing but this bird, which had somehow killed itself against one of the Lawn House windows. It was a pretty bird, olive brown and soft, but looking at it for hours and hours was too long in Edie's opinion. In the first place, she was sorry for it, and in the second, it ought to be buried. Chris carried it around on her palm, and Lou followed her wherever she went. Indoors and outdoors they took the bird. It bound them to a sort of quietness and good behavior, except that it excited Widgy into hysterics whenever he saw it.

"You get that dog away," said Chris, holding her hand high in the air. "We're waiting for this bird to rise from the dead, and we don't want him around."

Widgy, however, was determined to stay around. When Edie shut him up, he howled. If any birds were going to rise from the dead, he wanted to see such a thing.

"I don't think birds do, though," said Edie cautiously.

"Everything rises from the dead," Chris said. "Hood said so."

"That's not till Judgment Day. You can't wait *that* long."

"I'm going to wait till the end of the world to see this bird," said Chris.

She meant to do it, too. No more training, no more hardening, no more adventures, no more horses or heifers or fun, and Lou meant to stay with her. They would not come to lunch unless the bird was allowed to come, too. It lay between them on the table staring up from one blind eye, and Lou with her spoon clenched by her front teeth soothed it lovingly with her finger. After lunch they found a basket in the flower room and carried it out to the front steps. They could not be distracted by promises about games or a walk or even a hint that they could pretend to drive the Ford. They huddled on the cold stone as if they were birds themselves. Edie had to get their coats. After that she had to sit with them.

"We're not going *any*where without this bird!"

Edie would never have thought that Susan could ever be a beautiful sight, especially in the baggy old green sweater she wore lately and ragged sneakers with her toes showing through, but she was that afternoon as she came strolling up the back drive. And she would never have thought Susan could have a good idea except about rabbits, but almost as soon as she had been told about things and taken a look at the bird, she said: "Why don't you take him to the cemetery where he can rise with other people?"

"Dead people?" said Chris.

"Well, he *is* dead, you know."

"No!" said Chris. "This bird is going to *rise* from the dead, and we're going to see him."

"Only his soul," said Susan, having still another good idea, "not his feathers. And you can't see souls. They're invisible."

Even Susan couldn't do any good with somebody as obstinate as Chris.

"I'm going to," Chris said. "I'm going to see the soul of this bird."

"So'm I," said Lou.

Edie was surprised to have an idea herself just then. Ever since she had become a Good Samaritan about Madam's children, she had wondered if she were getting "softening of the brain" like Cook's aunt in Roxbury.

"Souls are ghosts," she said, delighted to think of it. "I suppose you know that. Do you want to see a ghost?"

Lou quickly put her thumb in her mouth. "Take that old bird away," she said thickly. She gave the basket a push with her foot.

"All right, I will," said Chris, getting up. "And don't you come with me. You're old pickled pie-faced peanuts, and you leave me and this bird alone."

Edie thought they ought to follow her, but Susan thought they ought not. "She's going to hide it somewhere," she said. "Let her. I bet we can find it later and get it buried. Little kids don't know anything about hiding. My brother hides things all the time in plain sight."

"Chris is a lot brighter than your brother," said Edie before she could stop.

"Is zat so," said Susan.

She got up as if to go, but Edie could not lose Susan, not this afternoon.

"Anyway, *you're* awfully bright," she said. "Especially today. When she comes back, let's take them to the Main Dairy and let them put their hands in the calves' mouths. I bet that would interest them."

She found she was completely mistaken. They had been chased by wild heifers and were not going near them again.

"They're only little calves," said Edie.

"They're pickled pie-faced peanut *cows*," said Chris, who had returned, "and we don't like 'em."

"Well, what *would* you like?" said Susan.

"We would like to see that bird—"

"Oh, shut up," said Edie, not able to stand it one more minute.

But she had to until another beautiful sight came up the back drive. It was Jane, slapping her riding crop against her boot. "I'll take them early tonight if you like," she said. "I haven't anything particular to do."

Oh, blessed day! Oh, my lovely sister! Oh, jumping frogs! Oh, moons and stars! "Susan, let's get *out* of here!"

It hardly took them five minutes to find the bird. Chris had left it in the little grove of tall pines beyond the back door and sprinkled a few pine needles over it. They took it to the small family graveyard beyond the row of maples and buried it among some laurel bushes there. Its grave was between Aunt Isabelle's baby and a cousin so young Edie had never even heard of him.

"It's a good place," said Susan. "He'll have some children to play with when he wakes up."

"If he likes *that!*" said Edie.

She walked home with Susan and Susan walked half-way back with her and she walked half of that back with

Susan. Finally there was a tremendous moon coming up as she went back toward the Lawn House alone. She meant to spend the rest of the evening "moon strolling" far, far away from any children. She meant to, but after dinner the house was so quiet that she walked upstairs with her eyes closed and undressed with them closed and groped herself to bed without once opening them, and promising herself that she would brush her teeth twice in the morning, she fell flat asleep.

She thought she had been asleep only about ten minutes when someone spoke to her. It couldn't be morning, so she wouldn't open her eyes. When the voice kept on speaking, she got under the covers. Nothing was going to make her open her eyes. If the house was on fire, someone else would have to save everybody and put it out. She couldn't. She *wouldn't*.

But the voice kept on buzzing. Of course it was Jane. Why couldn't she go away? "I'm asleep," said Edie. "I can't hear you."

There was one good thing about Jane. If she had to wake you up, she did it without shouting in your ear or pulling off the bedclothes, but she had no right to do it at all. Just the same, the voice came through.

"Edie, you have to wake up and answer. Do you know where Chris is?"

Edie flung herself over. Jane was there all right in her nightgown with her hair on end.

"No," Edie said. "I've been asleep. What are you talking about? You took her. *I* didn't do anything. What's the matter?"

"Chris isn't in bed," said Jane.

"Maybe she's in the bathroom."

"No. I've been all through the house. Is Widgy here?"

"He's under the bed." She looked, and a black nose came out to greet her. "Nobody's there but him," she said.

"You have to help me," said Jane. "Everybody's asleep and I don't want to frighten them, but we have to find her. Get dressed in your jodhpurs. It's wet. And bring Widgy. We'll have to look outdoors."

As Edie got dressed, she thought she must be having a dream. How could Chris disappear? She shivered all over from coldness and from having to wake, and a little because of Chris. "Widgy, go get her, good dog," she said with her teeth chattering. "You find her! Whist!"

Jane was in the hall, dressed, and they went out together, closing the front door softly. The moon was nearly at the top of the sky.

"You take one side of the house and I'll take the other," said Jane. "She might be hiding in the bushes somewhere. But why? Do you know why? What did you do today? She never got up before. She's scared of the dark. What on earth happened to her?"

"Maybe she turned into a bird and flew away," said Edie.

As she stumbled around the house, she couldn't rid herself of the idea. But where did birds go at night? Nobody in the world knew that. Except maybe about owls. Chris certainly hadn't turned into an owl; she wasn't wise enough.

Edie and Jane met on the terrace.

"Did Hood ever say she walked in her sleep?" Jane whispered.

"She never told *me*," said Edie.

"She never tells anybody anything about these kids," said Jane crossly.

"*I'm* telling you, she might have turned into a bird, but you don't pay any attention."

"You're still asleep," said Jane. "Come on, we better go to the stables. Was she in love with any of the horses?"

"Certainly not," said Edie. "She was only in love with this dead bird." Edie stopped in her tracks. "We could look in the place she hid the bird."

"Why didn't you say so before," said Jane. "Did you know there was an old well around here? It belonged to an old house that used to be beyond the pine grove."

Edie led the way, running to the pine grove. Of course, she should have thought of this place before. She could almost see Chris sitting there on the pine needles mourning about the bird, or crawling around on her hands and knees looking for it. She was sure as they came near that she heard Chris at that spot. It was shocking that she was not there.

"I heard her," said Edie.

"You!"

"We'll have to fly," Edie said. "Then we'll find her."

"If you don't stop," said Jane, "I'll slap you. That'll wake you up."

It was funny that Widgy would not come away from the pine grove. She might be still half asleep, but this Edie knew: Widgy thought there was something there, and he kept looking for it. It wasn't for the smell of the dead bird either. He wouldn't stay in one place at all. He kept lifting a paw and listening, here, there, and other places. Edie knew what it meant. She knew all about

Widgy. He heard something just as she had, and he kept on hearing it. He wasn't half asleep and dreaming. Then from somewhere in her dream or out of it, Edie herself heard the kind of noise birds make at night—a sort of gulp. Widgy barked like mad.

"Hear that?" said Edie. "It's a bird and it's Chris. She's flown up a tree."

"Look, Edie," said Jane quietly, "you go on in and go back to bed. There's a lot of places I have to go. It's bad enough just the way it is. I don't want someone who's walking in their sleep telling me things."

When Edie had finished yawning, she leaned against a tree. Nothing was farther from her mind, she said, than going back to bed. She just wanted to close her eyes a minute. "I'm going to fly up and get her," she said. "Just give me time to wake up and decide which tree."

When there was another gulp, Widgy decided for her, and Edie, propping up her eyelids, went to the tree he was yapping under. "It's this," she said, patting it. The tree was only a black mass against the moon, but there was certainly swallowing from the top. "I'm going up it."

"If you do!" said Jane.

"Watch me," said Edie.

She tore her arm away and was on the lower branches in a second. Jane caught her leg. "I'll kick." She knew the tree, she knew every branch and twig. It was probably the only tree for miles around that had any lower branches left, and the black cat often got stuck in it because he was afraid to back down.

"Jane, let go. I'm all right now. I'm *climbing*. Jane! I know this old tree. Let *go*." She gave her foot a flip and felt Jane's hand slide slowly off. Then she went steadily up hand and foot after hand and foot. She climbed almost as high as the black cat ever came. The moon was beginning to show through the branches. She tipped back her head. There was something just above her, but it was black.

"I thought it was a gigantic owl," Edie told Jane later. "It was just black against the moon."

It was Chris, though, up there in her nightgown, and when she came up beside her, Edie saw that she was just like the black cat—frozen scared. She couldn't speak or open her eyes. She kept her head down in her shoulders while she hung onto a branch beside her and kept shivering all over.

"Gee," thought Edie. "Can I manage it? Maybe we better get the fire department."

But Father always said he wasn't contributing to the fire department to get things out of trees. At least she'd better try. The first thing was to wake Chris up. She said her name. No answer. Chris wouldn't even open her eyes.

"If you do what I say, you'll be all right," said Edie.

"No," said Chris in a whisper.

Clinging to her own branch, Edie put out a hand to feel Chris's fingers. They were like steel. "If you let me take one hand, I can hold you while you find another branch," she said.

"No," said Chris.

Edie sat still a minute, her legs curled together. She felt steady, but she needed one hand in order to be perfectly steady, and the other wasn't enough to pry Chris loose. But she couldn't leave her. She was sure she ought not to leave her. Perhaps they would have to sit there till morning. She had better tell Jane.

"I can't move her," she called down. "She's here, but I can't make her do anything. She's too scared."

"Edie," said Jane, right at her feet. "I can't go any higher. I'm too heavy. Just take her wrists if you can and let her go. She'll slip right onto my arm, and I'll hold her till you go down and get under me."

Jane, who wouldn't stand on a stepladder!

It was really the easiest thing in the world once they got started, but to start Edie had to slap Chris on the face. That was easy, too. She was so mad at her that she wanted to slap her all over. Chris behaved just like the cat. She raised her head, spat at Edie, and tried to scratch with her free hand. Edie caught it and held on. Very slowly Chris got some sense in her white face. The moon flickered on it, and Edie could see it changing.

"Jane is *right there*," she said.

Chris dared to look. "Turn around," Edie ordered.

Good old Chris. When she wasn't crazy or something, she could do exactly as you told her. She didn't have to use Edie. She put her hands on the branch she was sitting on and lowered herself enough for Jane to find a place for her feet.

"Got her," said Jane. "Now, Edie."

Edie circled the tree like a squirrel.

"Let her come," she said.

Chris was all right now. She was more than all right. Halfway down the tree she slipped away from them and raced down by herself hand below hand. She stood on the ground looking up as they came after her.

"He did rise," she said, just before Edie jumped from the last branch.

"What?"

"He did rise. I went to look and he'd gone, but I heard him, so I climbed up, and I saw him up there, but his soul's not white, it's black. You don't know much about souls, I guess."

Late Saturday morning, Edie went whirling around and around down the back drive of the Lawn House as if she were a dervish. She crossed the swamp, almost running, without missing a single tuft, and she sang all the time at the top of her lungs: "And all the sweet potatoes even started from the ground-ound-ound-ound, and *all* the sweet potatoes even started from the ground. *While* we were march*ing* through *Georgia*." Of course, she stopped that before she got to Susan's. She simply swaggered across Susan's lawn instead as if she *were* singing it. Susan as usual was catching rabbits. After half an hour crawling around in bushes and under the piazza, the rabbits were all in their yard again, but Edie felt some of herself had been wasted.

"Why don't you fix it so they can't get out?"

"I do," said Susan. "I think I do, but they *love* it so, I can't resist leaving some holes."

They sat in the rabbit yard after they had taken what was left in the Stoninghams' cake box and talked about holes for rabbits.

"They must seem like miracles," said Susan.

Edie agreed with her. In fact, she had come over because she thought it only fair to tell Susan that she now believed in miracles herself.

It was because Father all by himself had revived an old law. Everyone had to take his turn; that was it, the law.

Edie could remember it herself. When she was five, *she* had been taken care of by Ted himself. "It was awful," she said. "Nobody ever knew if he'd kill 'em or not." Now, Ted and Hubert had to take their turn with Chris and Lou, and Edie and Jane were set free, just as it used to be. Was that a miracle or wasn't it? "A whole two days early!" More than that—Madam was coming home tonight; and she was better, much better, Father said.

And here was one more wonder. This morning she had reminded Chris that Hood would be home on Monday.

"That old Hood," Chris had said, taking a long suck of milk through a straw Gander had found for her and letting most of it dribble back into the glass. "We can never do anything when she's around."

Three

✤

THE HUNT

"Don't ask me what to do about her," Hubert Cares said to his brother, Theodore. "I'm only seventeen. How do I know about girls who go bats?"

"I wouldn't go so far as to call her bats," said Theodore. "Every once in a while she shows good sense, but she's always running off the field. It's our duty to keep her in, so she won't make a fool of herself."

"Or us," said Hubert.

Theodore tipped back his head and gave a little cough.

They thought they were alone in the Lawn House library on a Sunday afternoon. Jane was out, Madam had gone off to Florida with Chris and Lou, and Father had gone to New York for the weekend. They would have been alone, for Edie would certainly have been outdoors on this good October day if Widgy had not been sick under the library table. He had been eating bones as usual, Edie could see, but Father did not like a dog to throw up on the library rug, even when it was nice clean bones. So Edie had gone to the pantry at once, gotten one of Gander's good absorbent dish towels, and done such a good job that she could only see a small, small wet spot where the bones had been. She was just going out to bury the bones and the dish towel when the boys came in. Then, because it sounded interesting, she thought she would stay. The table was against the back of the sofa, and hardly anyone ever came around that side.

"It's a mystery to me," said Theodore, "how they always manage to do the wrong thing."

"Who?"

"Females, you ass."

"Oh, I don't know," said Hubert. He stretched out his legs and patted his hollow stomach. "Jane let me have her horse this morning."

"Very exceptional," said Theodore. "She probably had a bellyache."

He stretched *his* legs and put back his head again. It was really too much, he thought, that a mosquito like Edie should be allowed to run riot all winter without let or hindrance. She had begun right away, he wished Hubert to know. Just because she had been told in no uncertain terms to get out of the billiard room when he and his friend Dumbo Dalton had been playing an important match last weekend, she had taken a terrible dislike to poor Dumbo. The poor dumb guy couldn't understand it. He was quite a success with kids. And he had been unsuspicious enough to go to sleep on the billiard room couch. Edie, tiptoeing around in her sleuth-like way, had seen him, gone and gotten a scissors, and with one lightning chop cut off half of his elegant mustache.

"If she had only done it straight," said Theodore. "I told him she had probably tried not to get his nose, too, but it didn't console him. He had to take it all off and expose his juicy upper lip."

Theodore had to get up and pace up and down the library.

"There is apparently," he said, "not the most rudimentary sense of decency in girls. Now, with Madam gone, she's off on a new tack. She and that fat friend of hers, Susan Stoningham, have got religion. Did you know that?"

"Haven't seen a sign of it," said Hubert. To tell the truth, he could not remotely imagine Edie having anything to do with God, or God with Edie, until the Judgment Day, when there would be sheep and goats and Edie would just have to take it.

"How lately have you been to the corral boxes?" said Theodore, standing in front of him. "Just go," he said. "Take a look, take a smell, take a good satisfying smell of ten mangy dogs and five cats shut up in the old stalls. Wherever you put your foot these days, you get a howl or meow. You know what she said? She said: 'We're being Good Samaritans and rescuing these animals. Would you mind getting out of here?' "

"Fairly fresh," said Hubert, "but who lets her do it? Where's Pat these days?"

"He's under her thumb. Everyone's under her thumb. Don't ask me why. I can't think of a single good reason why anybody would want to do anything for a female half-wit with God on the brain. Ever since that suffrage parade, she and God are just like that." Theodore crossed his fingers.

"How do you know?" said Hubert. He was getting tired of Ted. "I never heard her mention Him in my life."

"All right," said Theodore. "I'll tell you. I let them all out. I gave the poor stinking brutes their freedom. Do you know what she said *then?* 'As soon as I get big enough, the wheels of God will grind you up.'"

"Fairly bats," said Hubert, "but why not take it easy?" To him it seemed a much better idea to have the mange and fleas shut up than jumping about the place.

"All right, all right," said Theodore, starting toward the door, "but when we are all scratching with ringworm, don't blame me."

"We wouldn't think of it, sweetheart," said Hubert. "We would just love you the more."

He had only lately been able to make such remarks to his Lordship and was trying them out once in a while. He wasn't sure they meant anything, but he was sure they were going to. He was an inch taller than Ted now and next year would be heavier. He ate constantly with this in view.

"So shut up and give the kid a chance," he said rashly. But he purposely did not get up. If Theodore thought of attacking, it would be easier to stop him with his feet.

After a look, Theodore left. He had played the foot game himself. Hubert wasn't worth saving. He never had been. He was always seeing so many sides that he never knew which one he was on. Theodore went riding and jumped his gray mare over the biggest gates he could find. She had not been exercised all week. It had taken Pat and Mike, the stableboy, as well as Cook and Gander, to get Madam off to Florida with her trunks, bags, boxes, hampers, medicines, children, and Hood, who thought it wasn't her place to do anything useful. The Troupial, Madam's wicked bird, had had to go—no one would take

care of him here—and the fox terrier, Jipp, so no one had
had time to take out the mare. She was wild, but Theodore liked that. He soothed and petted her before he set
her at the jumps.

Under the library table, Edie had to wait and wait for
Hubert to decide what he was going to do. When that was
nothing, she began to come out slowly and cautiously.
Hubert opened one eye. It stared at her. Then he closed
it.

"If I were you, I wouldn't mind *him*," he said.

"I'm going to make a war," said Edie, "so maybe I won't
mind you either."

"You are?" said Hubert, yawning till he was nearly inside out. "What on?"

"Men!"

"Great heavens!" said Hubert, sitting up quickly. "Well,
just remember I've always been on your side."

Monday was always a good day, rain or shine. The boys
had gone back to their old schools; Father went to business by an early train. Jane usually exercised her horse,
and Edie right after breakfast walked either across the
swamp, jumping from tuft to tuft, or along the avenue, if
she thought she might see a woodchuck, to Susan's. The
best arrangement in the world had been made about
school. It was so good that Edie thought she might have
made it herself. She and Susan had school in the Stoninghams' attic, and their teacher was one of the masters from
Grandfather's school. His name was Gibbs, and the Stoninghams had been able to get him because he was taking a
rest from having tuberculosis.

"And if I'm any prophet," Hubert had said when he heard it, "he'll have it again very shortly."

Like Mr. Silas Applegate Parker, who had lived with them at the beach last summer when Father and Madam were abroad, Mr. Gibbs read books all the time and only required that she and Susan read, too. It was the best and easiest way, he said, to acquire knowledge. They agreed.

In fact, things were turning out just right about staying at home. In the afternoons, every single afternoon, they rode through the woods of Aunt Charlotte's demesne. Susan's family, in spite of what the Bible said about giving, would not give her a pony, so Father, who never went to church at all, had done it instead. Edie mentioned this, but Susan said it had nothing to do with religion—it had to do with money.

"And it's a good thing your father had the chance," she said. "Maybe it will get him through the eye of the needle."

Edie had been ready to fight about this. She wasn't sure Father would get to Heaven, but she wasn't going to have him pushed in by Mr. Stoningham.

Susan wouldn't fight as usual.

"Oh, come on," she said. "I don't care how your old father gets into Heaven. I just said it because you were getting haughty."

Anyway, they had the ponies and could become what they were really meant to be—a gentleman jockey and the owner and trainer of wild horses from the western plains. Susan had wanted to be a jockey, too, but Edie said it was impossible if she had to wear her brother's old pants.

"It's all I've got," said Susan. "We're *poor*."

"You can't get into and out of everything all the time just because you're poor," said Edie. "You'll have to be a trainer."

They not only rode in the woods but also schooled their ponies over a small steeplechase course Theodore and Hubert had made in the Milldale Pastures. They did their best to persuade the ponies to jump the Sewertax gate, which the ponies refused to do, no matter how many times, by Theodore's advice, they threw their hearts and themselves over first. They raced each other across the Twenty Acre Lot as soon as the hay was cut and carted. Also they played games—especially the one of finding the tree with the brightest leaves and then an even brighter tree and a brighter one still and one still brighter.

This Monday morning was not raging with brightness as the world had been for weeks. The outside leaves had blown off, and inside there were little trees and bushes shining with gold pieces. Edie liked having school in Susan's attic, but as she crossed the swamp, which had turned orange and was edged with scarlet blueberry bushes, she wished she were a hunting dog on the scent of a fox, or better, much better, a hunter snorting with excitement just before he was allowed to break after the hounds, or best of all, a black panther padding the forest, slapping down monkeys.

At recess, she and Susan sat cross-legged on an old piece of carpet in Susan's rabbit yard. The carpet was on account of their clothes. Mrs. Stoningham was particular about clothes, but not so particular as Cook was at home about the kitchen. Mrs. Stoningham always said: "Take what you can find." So they had made a delicious new drink of cocoa and grape juice and had taken four frosted cup cakes out of the cake box. They each held a rabbit. Susan was gone on rabbits, and each one, every day, had to be petted.

Edie declared her war.

Susan leaned forward. "Did you say war?" she said. "Who on?"

"Men."

"I thought you'd done that long ago," said Susan.

Before Edie could even explain, she began objecting. She said it wasn't Christian; she said she and Edie were too young and too small; she said hate was wrong; she said her family wouldn't like it on account of bad manners. After all, she didn't think men were so bad. Her older brother had just given her twenty-five cents.

"All right," said Edie, "I'll do it by myself. But I'll tell you one thing. There won't be any rabbits in heaven— they make too much mess—so you'd better come to hell with me."

"Oh, dear," was all Susan said. "And they'd look so cute with wings." Susan, at times, was really awfully silly.

The war began very nicely. Edie started it, after recess, against Mr. Gibbs.

"How many pounds in a bale of hay?" she said to his back when he had turned to face the wall with his poetry book.

"Look it up in the dictionary when you get home," said Mr. Gibbs over his shoulder as quick as a wink.

It made Susan giggle, but she giggled at almost anything.

The next morning Edie kept it up.

"I couldn't find anything about bales of hay in the dictionary," she said. "Why don't you teach us arithmetic?"

Mr. Gibbs flipped some pages. "You're girls," he said.

Susan even giggled at that.

"How many inches in a foot?" Edie asked. "How many feet in a bottle, how many bottles in a can, how many cans in a wagon?"

Susan kept on giggling, but this time Mr. Gibbs did not answer and did not move. He turned pages regularly and interestedly as if he couldn't hear. Edie got up quietly, tiptoed to the window, and dropped out the *Tom Sawyer* they were supposed to be copying. She dropped out one by one all the books on the table. Then they had to sit with nothing to do for a whole hour.

"What's the use of that?" said Susan afterwards. "I got bored."

"He didn't like it either," said Edie. "I could see. And he had to pick up the books. And your mother saw him."

"Are you sure you're not a little bit loony?" said Susan.

At home Edie set a slight trap for Father by putting Hubert's false ink blot on the library rug, and while he was scolding Gander, she picked it up and held it out to him on the palm of her hand.

She tried some other things on Father, like eating pie with a spoon and swallowing prune stones, until the boys came home and they noticed.

"I suppose you think you're smart," said Theodore.

"Girls *are* smart," said Edie.

"Edith!" said Father, lowering the Sunday paper. "Behave!"

"No!" said Edie. "You are *nothing but a man.* Look," she said to Theodore, sticking out her tongue. There was another prune stone on the end of it. She closed her mouth and gulped. "Presto, chango, now look." She stuck out her tongue and the stone was gone.

"If I were you, sir," said Theodore, "I would just let her go to the devil in her own way."

"Just where I thought of going myself," said Edie. After that she thought it just as well to leave the table, but she took with her two large pieces of toast covered with jam. Did Their Majesties think she was going to starve?

Lots of people tried to save her. Aunt Charlotte came to look her over once more and asked her if she wanted to drive her father mad.

"Yes!" Edie said, and while Aunt Charlotte was still in the house, she tied a piece of meat to a string and lured the Chinese guardians into the coat closet and shut them up there. When they couldn't be found, Aunt Charlotte nearly went mad herself and told Father his Airedale must have eaten them.

Aunt Isabelle said that for her stepmother's sake she should try not to be such a nuisance to everyone. "It will worry her terribly to know that her dear little stepdaughter is causing so much trouble."

"Well, don't tell her," Edie said.

Cook and Gander gave her pieces of their minds every day.

"I'm not interfering with you, am I?" said Edie. "So why not shut up?"

It wasn't really true because she hid the key to the Ford, and Pat couldn't drive them to the Catholic Church on Sunday morning. Father had to drive them himself in the Packard. That Monday Edie told Susan the war was going very well.

"But I have to stop," she said sadly. "Mr. Carpenter's coming."

"Who's he?"

"A friend of Father's," Edie said. "But he's all right, just the same."

There were a whole lot of reasons why Mr. Carpenter could not be warred on. He was better than all right. He was dandy. He came to stay with them often because he had only a boat to live on and a cat called Penelope to live with him. His wife didn't like him, he said, and she didn't like Penelope either. "So when she picks up the rolling pin and advances upon us, we seek shelter on the hearthstone of a friend," he said. But he seldom brought Penelope. There were too many fierce canines about. He let her pick up a living in the vicinity of the boat.

"The ideal life," Hubert had said. "How can I get born again and be your cat?"

But Mr. Carpenter had not been in favor of Hubert turning into a cat. "Penelope," he said severely, "is a slave to duty."

That settled Hubert, who thought he had enough slavery on his hands just being at boarding school.

Mr. Carpenter had been seeking shelter with them for as long as Edie could remember. They had gone on expeditions with him in automobiles he sometimes had; Edie had been on a cruise in his boat; Theodore and Hubert had climbed Mount Washington with him and been caught in a blizzard. The best thing about him was that he just came and stayed, and whenever he did, something happened. The last time, it had been the mouse campaign. Mr. Carpenter hadn't been in the Lawn House that time for more than two days before he told Father that the place was infested with mice.

"Well, Harry," said Father, "I notice that since you came, the house has been infested with crumbs as well."

It was because Mr. Carpenter had to have a snack with his beer at eleven o'clock and another with his milk at night. Gander told everyone freely that she couldn't keep up with the man and his munching. But Edie munched with him and liked it very much.

So it was impossible to make war on a person like Mr. Carpenter, even if he was a man. Instead, she gave up riding for a few days and helped him to build a tree house in the big oak tree at the side of the Lawn House. It was big enough to lie down in and had a rope ladder that you could pull up after you. As a final touch, Mr. Carpenter cut hemlock boughs and matted the roof with them to keep out the rain. Looking up at it from below, Edie thought it good enough for a man from the Cannibal Isles.

"What's it for?" she said.

"Times of stress and strain," Mr. Carpenter said. "By pulling up that rope, perfect safety is achieved. No enemy, however swift and agile, could get at anyone in that house."

"Then it'll be my house," said Edie.

"It might," said Mr. Carpenter, "if the occasion arose. Here, you take one end and I'll take the other. Ladders are always awkward. Did I hear you were having a little trouble lately?" he said.

"Not me. Them."

"Now your father's a good man on the whole," Mr. Carpenter said, stopping walking. "And his life's not easy with your stepmother away. Why bother him so?"

"If I could have one victory," said Edie, "just one good victory, I'd be satisfied."

"Hmmm," said Mr. Carpenter.

They put the ladder away behind the barn and walked back to the Lawn House without any more conversation. Just before they got to the door, Mr. Carpenter took hold of his beard and looked down at her. "Your brother is giving a party here. Lots of fashionable ladies and their swains. November the twelfth, I believe."

"They won't invite me," said Edie quickly.

Mr. Carpenter pursed his lips. "Still, many things could be possible to one of your superior talents," he said.

There was so much secrecy going around the Lawn House every weekend after this that Edie felt it was her duty—well, almost her duty—to find out what was going on. Suppose Theodore and Hubert really meant to murder Cook because she gave them oatmeal for breakfast instead of fishballs and bacon and eggs. Suppose they really *had* decided to borrow Father's car and go to the Belmont Park races and lose all their money betting. She'd better know. The best place to hear was under the library table, but they had taken to looking there. The next best place was just around the corner, outside the library door. No one had thought of that yet.

All she found out was that the party His Lordship meant to give was really coming true. "Fashionable ladies and their swains" were coming to the Lawn House for the weekend, and there was to be a hunt on Sunday afternoon. Then that bad dog Widgy snuffed her out, and Hubert got up and found her.

"Walkie, walkie, little cat, how I wonder what you're at," he said, taking her arm and marching her down the hall.

"But what kind of hunt?"

He showed her the stairs and jerked his thumb at them.

"I don't see why I can't know what's going on in my own house," said Edie.

Hubert had grown lordly lately, too, and would not tell her. Neither would Jane who had been hearing it all, although Edie walked on Jane's heels, asking. Just one thing she did find out. She was right; she was not going to be invited.

If it had not been that Jane for some reason finally blew up and told the boys she would not have anything to do with their great plans and meant to go away for the weekend herself, Edie might never have known a thing and missed her one great chance. As it was, the boys tried to stop Jane. Ted even stood over her with the fire tongs, and Hubert took Father's glass paperweight away from her when she wanted to defend herself. But she would not give in. So they had to ask Edie to take her place.

"You're going to be a chaperone, my girl," said Theodore.

"What's that?" said Edie.

"You better keep out of it, Edie," said Jane. "They'll just get you in trouble."

"All you have to do is *be* here," said Theodore. "Jane is being a hen."

Edie thought so, too; she was only too delighted to be there. She would give up the war. She would forgive peo-

ple's trespasses, the way Susan said, and be helpful to her
neighbor.

The reason for all the secrecy, she found, was that Father at all costs must be kept from knowing. First, the
hunt was to be on Sunday.

"I don't think Father would mind Sunday," said Edie.

"You forget, my dear Edith, that your grandfather and
your Aunt Charlotte are still in residence," said Theodore,
"and they aren't so much holy as righteous."

Second, there was Dumbo Dalton. He had been forbidden the house. The last time he had come, he had sat
in Father's favorite chair, smoked his best cigars, and en-
gaged him in conversation about President Wilson until
Father had had to leave his uncomfortable seat on the
sofa, step into the hall, find Theodore, and tell him to
remove his long-winded friend before his day of rest was
entirely blasted.

Since, for the hunt, Dumbo was more or less the whole
show—it was he who had the friend who was bringing the
hounds—it would be "exceedingly dangerous," Theodore
considered, for him and Father to meet. And Father, Theodore had found out, was to be in New York that weekend, so it was all perfectly simple, if no one gave them
away.

"*I* won't," Edie said. "But what *kind* of hunt?"

Colonel Shepherd, Dumbo's friend, had a pack of beagles that needed exercise. He would bring them to the
Lawn House front door in a van at twelve o'clock on Sunday morning. The boys would be there to greet them,
after having had a small party the night before. "We
might dance a little," Theodore said. "You can look on if
you like." The beagles would be let out and then shep-

herded by Colonel Shepherd. They would trot down the drive until they smelled a rabbit, then whizzo, they would chase it, and the crowd would chase them. "I've seen it," said Theodore. "It's a lot of fun."

"And you, my dear," said Hubert, "may carry the rabbits."

Edie didn't know if he was being sarcastic or not, but she didn't care. She was asked to every conference the boys had. She was put in charge of the second floor, to see it had towels and soap for the ladies, and she was delegated to meet guests at the front door.

The weekend before the party, the conference had to be held in the barn tack room because it rained and Father never left the library all day long. It was very satisfactory, however. Theodore reported that by various wiles he knew, Cook and Gander had been brought into line.

"We now have to consider the kid's clothes," he then said. "So far as I have been able to observe, she hasn't any."

He turned thumbs down absolutely on the sailor suit she wore going to church with Grandfather. "It looks bad enough in a pew," he said.

Well, it was all there was. "I had some dresses last week," said Edie, "but by this time they're all too small."

Theodore's despair was so great that Jane said she would see about it. She even said she'd get a dress and pay for it herself. But that's all she would do.

"Then we're all set," said Theodore to Hubert. "I don't really see how anything can go wrong."

Edie, when it was time for the boys to start back to school, could not leave the front door, she was so sorry they were going.

When Jane came back from Canboro the next afternoon, she had found the dress all right. She had it with
her and showed it to Edie at once.

It was just right. It was made of dark blue velvet and
had nothing on it at all, not even a collar. Above it Edie's
yellow hair shone.

"You'd better wash it on Friday," Jane said.

"I *will*. Gee, Jane, thanks!"

When Edie got a letter from Theodore Thursday morning, she thought it must have more instructions, so she
took it out to the tree house to read. It was a warm November morning with no wind. Edie was thinking as she
looked out over the farm meadows that it was just the
kind of weather they said was good for hunting. She was
quite sure that no beagles could ever catch one of the
farm rabbits, and she was pretty sure that Theodore's
friends would never be able to keep up with beagles, but
it was going to be wonderful watching them try, especially as she knew perfectly well she could herself out-
distance them all. She crossed her legs, sat down, and was
ready to do whatever she was going to be told.

Ted's letter said:

"*Dear Edie:*

"You may think this is bad news, but then, since
like Jane, you're a girl, you may not. No chaperone.
I thought it was a good idea, but the chaps are doubtful. Don't forget Dumbo's mustache! Have got Harry
Carpenter to say he'll come. This will please the old
man when he's bound to hear. So you are relieved of
all responsibility, not to mention bother, and I'd
appreciate it if you'd make yourself a little scarce.

How about visiting your fat friend for Saturday night?

"If you and Jane bought the dress, you ought to have a decent dress anyhow.

"Come to the hunt if you want, but no showing off.

> "*Affectionately your brother,*
>
> *Theodore P. Cares.*"

For just one minute Edie couldn't move; then not even looking at the rope ladder, she jumped from the tree house. It was ten feet and it hurt her ankles, but she didn't feel it. She rushed for the front door. Jane had left a basket of vegetables there that she had brought up from the root cellar. Edie grabbed them up, lugged them into the front hall, and slung them bumping and rolling—beets, carrots, parsnips, turnips, and a squash—all over the floor. She raced upstairs, raced from room to room till she found a pair of scissors, Jane's nail scissors, then went to her closet and cut small round pieces out of the blue velvet dress until it was covered with small dark holes. The third thing she did was to run down to the swamp to go to Susan's. She couldn't stop. If she did, her life would stop, too. She forgot about Widgy who came panting after her. She was panting herself, so she could hardly breathe by the time she got to the Stoninghams' wall and found Susan had gone off and no one was there. "Oh-oh-oh," she said, pounding the wall. She would have to begin running again. She started down the road a little like a mad dog, steady and straight, but swerved off as a car came along to get to the lane that led to the Summerton swimming hole. The driver swore at her and nearly stopped.

"Yah," she said to him under her breath. "I'd like to see you catch me."

She ran stumbling and tripping and panting down the uneven lane and, when the pool was in front of her, saw that it was just a black mud puddle, drained for the winter.

"I wasn't going to jump in anyhow," she said to it. "Anyhow, I can swim. Anyway, I have to get Theodore. Anyway, I have to have revenge."

On the way home she stopped at the stables. If she could have had a wish, she would have made the Lawn House disappear and gone to live in the woods forever, so she put off going back to it. Pat was watering and pitching hay, and she stayed a little while to watch, and when he had combed his white hair before the cracked mirror by the trough to go up to breakfast, she walked with him.

"There's to be great doings, I hear, Miss, over this weekend," he said.

"Yes," said Edie.

"Them little dogs, now," he said, "would they be catching anything, I wonder?"

"They chase rabbits," said Edie.

"And where would they find them?" He looked down at Widgy. "Sure your own great hunter here have every rabbit run out of the neighborhood." He stopped to ruffle Widgy while he talked. "Why wouldn't that brother of yours have a drag hunt while's about it and have some real sport?"

"What's a drag hunt?" Edie asked.

"You've heard of them, Miss, for sure. A ball of scent on the end of a rope dragged across the country. The hounds is after it like greased lightning and never let up till they come to the end."

"Oh," said Edie. "Oh, I have heard of them. Would it work for beagles?"

"And why not?" said Pat. "Good morning now, Miss. Just get my words to Mister Ted, he'd best have a drag. There isn't a rabbit between here and the Milldale Pastures."

"I will," said Edie. "Oh, I will."

At school later, Edie was stupider than even Mr. Gibbs could stand, and he sent her out of the attic to sit on the floor in the hall "until she could find her brains," he said.

"I left them at home," said Edie, "where they're needed."

She had gotten them back by recess enough to explain to Susan about drag hunts and how they could be used. Of course, Susan at once objected. She thought God ought to take care of revenge. Edie said that she could not wait for ninety years. Susan still thought God ought to do it.

"Did you ever hear of the Little Red Hen?" said Edie. "God got somebody to write the story, you know."

Susan's objections grew weaker after this and were not so much about God as about how they were going to do things.

"I must say I never heard of a scent called 'rabbit'," she said. "Are you sure there is one?"

"It's not *called* 'rabbit'," said Edie. "It just smells like rabbit."

"Well, it's a good smell," Susan said, snuffing the one she held. "Probably any hound would like it, but I bet you won't be able to buy it in Summerton."

"I'll bicycle to Canboro," said Edie. "They sell it at a hardware store. You can be making the bag. I can't sew. Make it good and big. We'll stuff it full and pour on the whole bottle."

Susan had one more objection.

"Suppose they catch us?"

"They won't. They'll all be snoring. It's hardly daylight by half past five, and nobody at my house gets up on Sunday morning, not even the dogs."

"Well," said Susan, dumping her rabbit as Mr. Gibbs rang his bell, "all I can say is, I hope it's a brighter idea than any you've had so far this morning."

"It's *the* brightest I ever had," said Edie. "It's brighter than Bull Run or Manassas," she added, remembering that Susan's grandfather came from Cambridge, Maryland, and Susan was proud of it. "It's as bright as General Lee."

"He got beaten," said Susan quickly.

"Then it's as bright as Ulysses S. Grant," said Edie.

When Edie left to visit the Stoninghams on Saturday morning with a suitcase in one hand and her riding boots in the other, she left a note propped against the big vase on the big hall table.

"Dear Ted," it said.

"I'm making myself scarce the way you said. We're very pleased to accept your kind invitation. See you at the hunt.

"Your loving and admiring sister, Edith M. Cares."

"Just the same," said Hubert, while he was looking over Theodore's shoulder as he read it, "if I were you, I'd examine all the beds, especially your own."

"The meek have cheek," said Mr. Carpenter, pursing his lips and whistling under his breath.

Theodore was pleased with it. "She seems to be learning a little tact," he said.

Just as a precaution, Mr. Carpenter went out and squinted up at the tree house. It was silent and dark.

"Peace and prosperity seem to have descended on this house," he said as he came in. "May all be well."

All was very well until five-thirty on Sunday morning, and then the only people who were uncomfortable were Susan and Edie. It was terribly cold and, although it hadn't rained lately, dampish. They could tell that later, when the sun would be really up, the whole ground would be covered with a white frost. Edie tried to be cheerful.

"I've heard it's just the right kind of day for scent," she said.

"Well, let's hur-rur-rurry," said Susan, trying to get the bridle on Thomas Aquinas while she was shaking all over.

After all, it did not take long, and there was just one moment of danger. They had to start the drag near the house in order to be sure the beagles would pick it up right away. If anyone were looking out the window— No one was. They had danced until two o'clock, and Mr. Carpenter had had to stay up, too, to chaperone faithfully. Edie dropped the scent bag not far from the front door, loosed the rope that dragged it, and they were off, not very fast, but to lots of places rabbits didn't usually go. There were even two or three places the ponies couldn't go. Edie got off and dragged the scent bag herself.

"What'll we do with the bag now?" Edie asked as they were coming back down the steepest hill of Aunt Charlotte's demesne behind the Lawn House barn.

"Could we drag it to your father's car, maybe?" said Susan just as if she were as well acquainted with the devil as Edie.

"I'll rub the cushions a bit, too," said Edie.

The sun was just up, and it was going to be the most perfect day. Not quite clear, but not cold any more, warmish, dampish, and sweet. Rabbit scent would last for hours.

"We hope," said Susan.

At exactly a quarter to eleven, they were hidden behind the wall that separated the Lawn House from the tract of little trees next door. How Susan had gotten off from church, Edie couldn't understand unless God Himself had arranged it. He must have somehow or other influenced Mrs. Stoningham. Edie had influenced Grandfather by saying she had been stung by a bee. They could see the Lawn House front door, and when it drove up, the van full of jumping beagles with Colonel Shepherd driving. After that, it didn't take long before Theodore and his friends came trooping out the front door. Dumbo Dalton talked to Colonel Shepherd and pointed across Aunt Charlotte's meadows.

"Just in the right direction," Edie whispered.

Next there was some shouting, Colonel Shepherd blew a horn, and Theodore yelled: "Everybody ready?" And a man in a green coat and velvet cap opened the back of the van.

Out came the little dogs and jumped neatly down. They did nothing, just wagged their tails and stayed clustered in the drive. Edie could hardly breathe. "Make it work," she said under her breath, "make it work." But with perfect manners the little dogs moved down the drive around

Colonel Shepherd and the man in the green coat. The crowd followed them, talking and laughing.

"We made a mistake," said Susan. "We dragged on the grass."

"Oh," said Edie, in a kind of moan.

Colonel Shepherd and Dumbo Dalton stopped for a minute, the crowd stopped, and the pack stopped, all but one good little dog who wandered off the drive and suddenly gave a loud ki-yi.

"He's found it," said Susan, "the darling. Come on, Edie, they're all going. We've got to go, too."

The first place they went was down the drive and then, screeching, down the Summerton Main Street just as church was getting out. The beagles and the congregation met head on at the bottom of the church lawn. It didn't bother the beagles a bit. They were all mixed up for a minute, and then the beagles came out on the other side and headed for the churchyard. The crowd slowed to a walk while Susan and Edie skirted around them into some bushes. "We're chasing a rabbit," they heard Dumbo Dalton say to Mr. and Mrs. Nathan, the postmaster and his wife. "Did you see a rabbit?" he shouted when Mr. and Mrs. Nathan seemed to be deaf.

He had to lead the crowd on without an answer. The church people stared after them speechless except for the minister, who came out on the church porch. "Shocking," he called in his loudest voice. "Shocking!"

The crowd was held up in the churchyard, where the rabbit had dodged among the stones. Edie had thought Susan would object to this, but no, she thought all animals should be able to go where they liked, when they liked, especially dogs. "And it'll be so nice for them," she had

said. Now it gave Colonel Shepherd a chance to blow his
horn, but the beagles didn't mind that. They had a fine
time sniffing and then shot out the back gate, turned left,
and raced down the hill past Miss Lydia Hardy's. She and
her cat, who were saying their prayers as usual by her
back wall, ran for it, the cat up a tree and Miss Lydia
for her kitchen door, holding her skirts. She needn't have
worried, as Susan and Edie could have told her. Neither
of them had wanted to disturb Miss Hardy. It was just
an accident; the beagles with their noses to the ground
wouldn't have looked at a hundred cats. They were only
interested in the delicious smell of rabbit, which was leading as straight as a string to Aunt Charlotte's front door.
There they stopped again, to paw and ki-yi. Theodore led
the straggling crowd, panting.

"Hey, call off your dogs," he was yelling all the time at
Colonel Shepherd. "Something's gone wrong."

Colonel Shepherd did not answer. He was too busy
kicking and flinging the beagles down the steps. But they
kept at it, and Wong and Mr. Wu began answering from
inside. So, finally, did Aunt Charlotte, who opened a window and stood majestically inside it. She tried to say
something, but no one heard her. There was too much
noise. Warren, the butler, opened the half door.

"Madam," he said, "has sent for the police," and closed
it quickly.

Behind one of Aunt Charlotte's big maples, Edie and
Susan doubled up.

Nothing would get the pack away until that one good
little dog—Susan's darling—again picked up the trail and
ki-yied. They followed him at once. "His name ought to
be Hero," said Susan. They shot over Aunt Charlotte's

lawn, through her lilac bushes, and were at Grandfather's in a second. Grandfather's cellar door just happened to be open, and down they poured. But the crowd by this time stood off and waited. Some of them were not there at all. They had gone back to the Lawn House from Aunt Charlotte's. Edie and Susan were there and came right up to the crowd.

"Never," said one lady to another, "never in my life have I seen beagles behave like this."

"The whole country must be a mass of rabbits," said her friend. "It shows how they need the beagles."

"But not on their doorsteps or in their cellars, do you think?" said the first.

The noise in Grandfather's cellar was frightful. The men in the party went down to try to stop it, and soon the beagles were being thrown out, one after the other, as if they were being exploded into the air. Grandfather came out and stood in his drive with his cane upraised.

"Are you responsible for this outrage, sir?" he said to Dumbo Dalton, who was nearest and had a beagle in his arms.

Dumbo could only open his mouth. "Then remove them from my dwelling," said Grandfather, shaking the cane, "and remove yourself from this vicinity. Theodore, can this be you? In such company? With this passle of wild women? For shame, sir. Be gone, the lot of you."

Edie and Susan sat on the road wall with their hands under them, crouched together with pleasure, but very meek and quiet and a little way off from the crowd. No one seemed to have noticed them at all. The little dogs went by them into the dusty road, and they were meek and quiet, too, and much pleased with themselves. Their tongues were hanging out and their sterns gently wagging.

"Let them find it once more, let them find it once more," Edie prayed, squeezing the stones.

Colonel Shepherd sat down and beat his horn against his thigh. The beagles sat down around him.

"You had enough?" Colonel Shepherd asked the red-faced ladies and their swains, who were mopping their faces.

"Plenty," someone said.

"There's something queer going on," said Colonel Shepherd. "Here, Dandy, stay by, boy. Jim, get back to Mr. Cares' and bring the van. I'm afraid to move. Dandy! Here, boy! Confound it, *catch that hound!*"

It was too late. Dandy raised his head, sniffed, trotted a little way. Every beagle got up and began searching. Dandy found the scent, and they were off again.

"Oh, the love!" said Susan.

This time they ran through the meadows where the milking cows were having one final bite of grass. The pack sent them galloping in every direction, their udders swinging.

"Cream cheese for supper," one of the ladies said to Theodore gaily.

"Double, double damnation," said Theodore.

The girls did not need to follow them this time. They could see everything that went on in the open fields, so they took a short cut up the hill. They would meet the hounds as they swung back toward home. It worked perfectly. Just as they reached the top of the hill, the beagles came racing on. No one followed them. The crowd had been left far, far behind, stumped by the sunken brook that ran across the meadows. It was a pity. The crowd was going to miss the final mystery of the beagles' dash for the barn and their pounce upon Father's car. It had been well soaked with rabbit, and the little dogs would be ecstatic. Edie and Susan watched them come, feeling sorry that they had made this one mistake. They had giggled a lot over the thought of the ladies and swains trying to jump the brook. Now, draggled and exhausted, they were trying instead to find the road, led by Theodore, who was throwing his hands here and there between Colonel Shepherd and Dumbo Dalton.

"Oh, what a glorious morning," said Susan. "It came out exactly right, didn't it?"

"Gee," said Edie. "Oh, *look!*"

The beagles were not turning to rush for the garage and Father's car. After slowing down a little and raising their noses, they were going straight ahead. What they were smelling, Edie and Susan saw. Father's car was not in the garage at all. It was standing at the curve of the drive, and Hubert and Father were standing beside it watching the view. It didn't take a second to know why. Father had come home early, and Hubert had gone to meet him. They must be covered with rabbit, and the hounds would just love them. Susan and Edie were paralyzed until Edie kneeled down and finally lay flat on the grass.

"Don't tell me," she said. "Don't tell me a thing about it."

She was not going to watch half her family being eaten up before her eyes. She could hear their bones cracking and the munching of the beagles.

"Don't be a goat," said Susan, sounding disappointed. "They've gotten into the car and are going up the drive.

But," she added in a brighter voice, "the whole pack is following them. Oh, the little loves!"

Edie could not stay at the Stoninghams' forever, although she and Susan agreed that that would be far the safest thing to do.

"Your brothers are suspicious people," Susan said.

Edie said she knew it, but what could she do about it? She had to go home sometime. "Your *mother* is getting suspicious, too," she added. Also, she had noticed that Susan herself had gotten wobbly. They had not waited to see Father overrun by beagles or to watch the arrival of Colonel Shepherd and Dumbo Dalton under the protection of Theodore.

They had disappeared, but as they were doing it, Susan had collapsed so badly that Edie didn't know if she could speak to her again the rest of her life.

Staying at the Stoninghams' was not exactly pleasant with Susan repenting out loud all over the place. Just before supper, Edie carried her small suitcase and riding boots back the way they had come. When she got home, she was surprised to find the Lawn House empty and silent. She looked cautiously in the downstairs rooms. There was no one in them. In the dining room the table was set for two people. Who were they? As she was going quietly upstairs, Mr. Carpenter appeared below her looking up and holding his beard.

"Where's everybody?" said Edie.

"They have fled," said Mr. Carpenter. "They have melted away."

"Father, too?"

"The iron," he said, "had entered his soul. I believe he

has gone to his club to expunge—I said expunge—both that and the smell of rabbit."

"Well, he can come back," said Edie. "I won't do another thing." She picked up her luggage. "At least for quite a little while."

Four

+-+- ❀ -+-+

THE KIDNAPER

If anyone had told Edie that she would ever be glad to leave Summerton, she would simply have answered: "I would rather be a skunk in this town than anything else, anywhere." She would not have seen what there was to laugh at. It was just the truth. And why not? As Hubert said: "She was being handed things on a platter." He did not mean jewels or automobiles or yachts or race horses; he just meant time and the weather. This year by Thanksgiving it had snowed a little, and as it had not yet frozen hard, there was plenty of mud with which to try the new door scraper. It worked beautifully, shirring off dirt like wood chips and then polishing up with its side brushes. By the first week in December it had snowed hard—soft snow that packed down—so that the roads were like white turf to gallop the ponies on, and just after this it froze, not a brittle freeze that broke and cut, but one that turned the whole countryside into a nice firm cake frosting. It could be walked on anywhere. It could be coasted on from almost the front door. Any little hill could be used, and the big ones made a sled go so fast that it was impossible to see, but that did not matter. Since the whole world was frosted, the sled could go where it liked except for trees and fences, and there were plenty of hills in Summerton where there were none until the long plain at the bottom. There was especially Aunt Charlotte's great sweep of meadow to the north of the Lawn House, where she had made sure that nothing would interfere with the cutting of her hay. The Cares family had used it for steeplechases, trapping woodchucks, finding larks' nests, practicing golf at the appropriate times of year ever since they could remember, but nothing approached the way Edie and Susan could use it when it was frosted over in this particular way. They started at one side of its deep steep bowl, gave their sleds their heads, and flew, simply flew, until they were nearly halfway up the other side. The walk to the top with their feet turned sideways was then almost nothing until they could turn and come down the other way. They were agreed that in the blue, white, golden air, it must be exactly like flying.

Besides this, Grandfather's school, with Hubert and Mr. Gibbs in it, caught the chicken pox. Hubert was sent home, but Mr. Gibbs was incarcerated. No school and no Theodore. On account of Theodore's suspicions, Edie had had to spend a great deal of time on weekends in her tree house or, when she wasn't there, "have eyes in the back of her head," as Hood so often remarked. Now all was well. Even if he had had suspicions, Hubert would not have done anything about them. He preferred trying to see what the Ford would do on the snow-covered roads. And Theodore was not going to expose himself to the danger of chicken pox, even to have revenge.

"It's not much of a disease," Edie said. She had had it.

"He's become something of a parlor snake, I believe," said Hubert.

Well, naturally, if Ted was sitting around holding girls' hands, he didn't want to be covered with spots. It seemed a foolish thing to do while Summerton was like this, and she almost relented toward him—after all he had not killed her in spite of his suspicions about the hunt, and he had said some pretty funny things about Dumbo Dalton— but the frosted weather did not last long enough for her to worry about it. She had exactly three days of being able to walk over the world about a foot higher than usual. Then it began to melt. Susan slid off her sled in a soft place and went along on her stomach and face for quite a way before she could stop, and Edie's knee, the one that sometimes went out of joint, almost did when she kept crashing through the crust unexpectedly.

After the thaw it rained, a measling, drizzling, nonstopping rain. Edie made the mistake of going to Susan's through it and found Susan was being punished for sloppiness in her room. She had to learn the 19th Psalm from beginning to end. She was sitting cross-legged on the bed, holding a rabbit, and the Bible was on the floor.

"You might as well learn it, too," Susan said, after she had explained. "It might do you some good in the spring."

She meant, Edie knew, that with Grandfather gone to town for the winter and no more church on Sundays for her, she could be storing up a little treasure in heaven. Susan hadn't noticed that Edie had done a single good deed lately either.

"Well, I've been with you most of the time," said Edie.

But she agreed to learn the psalm if Susan would stop being grumpy.

On the way home she felt already rewarded. God must have been paying attention. That measling, drizzling rain was beginning to freeze, and through the occasional Summerton street lights she could see the crystal coating that had begun. She knew what that meant—an ice storm. It was one of the things she had wanted to stay at the Lawn House, and in Summerton, to see. She loved ice storms. She went to bed feeling that tonight was better than Christmas Eve. On Christmas Eve, she could only hope she was going to get what she asked for. This night she knew she would.

In the morning, as soon as she opened her eyes, she realized the present she had expected was not quite right, and she hopped to the window to see what was the matter. The rain wasn't over. It was still keeping on in that misting, mizzling way. But maybe all the better, she thought. When the sun did come out, what a sight it would be! Everything would be turned to ice, as if they were all living in *The Blue Fairy Book*. She watched for the sun all day, hopping around on one leg so as to give her knee a rest and be ready for tomorrow. Looking out the window every so often to see how things were getting on, she approved of it all. The birch trees were bent double, the pines by the kitchen door hung their branches from top to bottom, the elm trees along the drive were looking like half-shut umbrellas, the meadows were covered with crystal spikes, and the drive was a sheet of glass. She called up Susan on the telephone and made an agreement with her to pray that the sun would be out in the morning. When Father called up to tell her he could not get home, she did not mind a bit, and when Jane wandered from window to window worrying, she told her for goodness' sake to stop.

"The trees," said Jane. "The trees."

"They're wonderful," said Edie. "I never saw anything like them."

It must have been Jane's gloominess that gave her nightmares. She often dreamed about Indians, and once she had been shot clear through by an arrow, but this time it was robbers and they had pistols. They kept shooting them at her no matter where she tried to hide. One shot was so loud that it brought her almost awake, but when she opened her eyes for a minute, there was the moon shining in the window. Everything was all right, so she did not stay awake long enough to get rid of the dream. The robbers were after her again, with their guns cracking, as soon as she went back to sleep, and when she was woken up by the sun flooding her windows because she had overslept, they were still cracking, in broad daylight. *What* was the matter? Were all the automobiles in the world backfiring on the Summerton hill on account of the ice? She hopped to the window to see if she could see them. She found that the crystal world she had expected was so dazzling with the sun on it that she couldn't see anything. She would dress while her eyes got used to the light.

From the downstairs windows she was able to look without being blinded. It was the most tremendous sight she had ever seen. She did not know what to do with it inside herself. It was not only that everything was covered with ice, which made it look as if it were hung with diamonds. The sun on it made a kind of light shine through from the very middle. From the Lawn House hill, it was just as she had thought it would be. She could see the whole countryside, every telephone pole—how delightful, they were all leaning drunkenly this way and that with their wires hanging dripping with icicles. She could see every meadow with the grass tipped over, every shrub, sheeted and shining, every tree—every t-r-e-e— what was the matter with the trees? Jane came and stood beside her.

"I don't know exactly what we're going to do," she said. "There's no water and no light."

"Why not?" said Edie sharply. If Jane could be gloomy, she certainly would be.

"Can't you *see?*"

Suddenly Edie could see, but more than anything she saw the trees. They were sticks with tufts at the top, bent spears, and in a circle around them diamond crowns made of their branches. Those were the pistol shots, the breaking to pieces of the trees! She could not speak, and Jane could not speak either. They could not even look at each other at breakfast. When Hubert came down, they did not raise their eyes to look at him.

"Phew," he said, "what a shambles! What'll we do?"

It made Edie think of the hurricane at the beach last summer. That had been kind of a shambles, too.

"Let's go out and see it," she said. If Summerton was a shambles, she wanted to look at it before the ice wore off. It was terribly beautiful, and besides that, it seemed to be terribly exciting to look at such a ruin.

The three of them left Gander's squawking about lights and Cook's moaning about water and walked all morning through the glitter and shine. There was not a car to be seen, even on Main Street. How could there be? The roads were blocked everywhere. They climbed and circled the great fallen branches and stayed well away from the light wires and poles. By the time they got back, hungry and exhausted, they felt they had seen almost every twig in Summerton and had done a kind of duty that should not have been avoided. It was true that Jane had kept saying: "We really ought to be—" Hubert and Edie knew as well as she did that Pat would need help about water for the horses and that Gander and Cook would be having a fit.

"Several fits," said Hubert. "But this is more important."

Even Jane had to agree. In the first place, it was something that had never happened before, and in the second, no matter what it had done, that supercolossal ice storm was the most beautiful sight that had ever come into their lives.

"You have to appreciate a thing like that," said Hubert.

In the third place, they found, they had almost not been needed—the girls, anyhow. Father had gotten home. He had come on the train and walked from the station, climbing over things himself. Just as if he had had a broom, he swept them all out of the Lawn House almost before they could say anything. None of them was to stay at home until the shambles had been cleared away and ordinary life resumed. Hubert was to help Pat, live in the room over the carriage house, and eat in the village. Gander and Cook were to visit relations, Jane was to go to Aunt Charlotte's, and Edie was to see if she could collect her friend Susan and then somehow be put on a train to Florida to stay with her stepmother till after the Christmas vacation.

"But what will *you* do?" Jane managed to ask before they were hustled upstairs.

Father meant to live at his club in Charlottesville until, with Theodore's help, they could see that things were restored to order.

By the time the girls and Father walked back to the station that afternoon lugging their suitcases, Summerton had begun to drip from everywhere, and its bare bones were showing through. They met Susan with her suitcase at the corner of Simms Road just above the station. Like them, she was quiet and did not look around very much. She and Edie sat shoulder to shoulder on a station bench, while Father got the tickets.

"We must have prayed too hard," Susan said, in a very low voice.

"*I* think it was just a mean trick," said Edie. If Susan thought she was going to let herself be blamed for this ice storm, she was much mistaken. She wouldn't have done such a thing to Summerton for the world.

"Well, look! We're going to Florida together."

"My father fixed that," said Edie firmly, "and *nobody* else."

Still, Susan could not get rid of the idea that God was being awfully good to them. She drew attention to it again as their train was pulling out of the Pennsylvania Station. "Look what we've got!" she said.

It was a compartment on the train to Palm Sands, Florida, a small house with an upper and a lower berth, where they were to live for three days, attended by a porter whenever they rang a bell and fed by him with heaped-up trays of sumptuous food whenever they so desired. "It's almost as good as 'Little goat, little goat, bring me my table.'"

"*That's* Cousin Lyman," said Edie. "He's head of this railroad, and he told Madam we'd be taken care of."

"God gave you your relations, you know," said Susan.

She thought she had won that argument, but Edie was still cross about the ice storm and perhaps still crosser from having been up very late the night before. She felt absolutely convinced that Susan should not be allowed to become either obstinate or holy—at any rate not right off, not right at the beginning of their trip.

"How do you know it wasn't the devil?" she said. "Look at Ted, for instance. Hey, will you please give me that handkerchief you stole from him. This seat is pricking my legs."

Susan would not think of it. Two people can be cross as well as one, and if Edie started being bossy the very second they got on their way, what would happen to the rest of the vacation?

Instead of glaring at each other, they glared out of the window at the New Jersey marshes. Edie knew all about that handkerchief. Susan had put it down her front as near her heart as possible because she was more in love with Theodore than ever, since he had brought them to New York, fed them amid the dazzling lights and silver of the Belmont Hotel, taken them to the circus, and today put them on the train with a bag of bulls-eyes, some snow apples, and "funny papers," without a single complaint.

"Maybe you don't know niceness when you see it," said Susan.

"Well, he was getting rid of us for three whole weeks," said Edie. "No wonder."

Susan suddenly broke down. What was the use of having a fight? The fact was, she said, it made her feel sick to think of such a sacred object being sat on. "And the truth is," she added, putting her hands under her own legs and giving a hiccup, "I've felt sick ever since breakfast."

"Lovesick, I suppose," said Edie, not unsympathetically. As long as Susan wasn't going to be obstinate and holy, she would do anything for her, and maybe this was the time to try out the porter's bell to see if it would be answered. She got up and started toward it but at once sat down again. Heavens! He might think they had on no underclothes, if they complained about the seat pricking their legs. So she dragged out her suitcase, rummaged for her pajama top, and spread it over the stiff plush. She offered to get Susan hers, but Susan laid her head back and said she didn't much care, but that she didn't think love ought to feel like a stomach-ache.

"Then it's probably peanuts," said Edie. "I've had that myself."

"I wish you'd shut up and let me go to sleep," said Susan.

The conductor, however, interrupted her slumbers almost at once by wanting to see their tickets and then by having to make conversation to Cousin Lyman's relatives.

"Traveling alone, eh, all the way to Palm Sands?" He peered at their tickets, which unfolded almost to his feet, used his punch in several places, tore off a piece, folded them up—very badly, Edie thought—and handed them back. Then he peered at *them*. "Ticketed and labeled, eh?

Good enough. The porter'll have his eye out for you, young ladies. Don't get off till the train stops. Ha. Ha." He thought this such a good joke that he said it again as he moved out into the rest of the car. It made Edie remember she had forgotten to take off the tags Theodore had put on them, with their names and addresses. Just as if they weren't able to talk! She did this now, Susan's, too, and slipped them down a crack near the window.

"Suppose there's a train wreck. They won't know our corpses," said Susan languidly.

"*You* shut up," said Edie.

"It's the way I'm feeling," said Susan.

Edie had no regrets about the tags. Susan would be recognized by her hair no matter how much she was mashed in a wreck, and she would love that. She had a thick gold braid, and on top it was a little curly. She was always flinging that braid around. Edie's own hair—short and yellow—would not be good enough to admire on the head of a corpse, but if she were dead, she bet she wouldn't care a nickel. Anyway, Cousin Lyman's trains didn't go fast enough to be wrecked. They crawled along past what looked like all the rubbish in the world. It was so boring that she got up to investigate the compartment. They were to be in it for three whole days *and* nights, and right now there did not seem to be anything interesting enough to last more than five minutes, especially if Susan was going to go on having stomach-aches. They had meant to start the trip with parchesi, which they both felt they had never played enough, and go on and on until they were stuffed with it, but they couldn't start yet. Widgy was in the baggage car. Edie was to go to visit him once a day. Theodore had seen to that, too. For once in

his life he had been in a good humor. In fact, he had let
them laugh so much at the circus that what Susan probably had was a laughing pain. Edie opened a door and
looked admiringly at the washstand and toilet, found the
porter's bell beside the door, turned all the light switches
on and off, and looked at their coats hanging swinging in
the coat closet. That was all there was to the compartment. Three whole days! Whee, what would they do?
Sometimes Edie wondered how she could *stand* Susan and
all the things she had the matter with her—religion, stomach-aches, and the way she loved Theodore. As she looked
at her now on the opposite seat, with her eyes closed and
her head hanging, not able to play parchesi or even talk,
she did not see how she was going to spend the whole
Christmas vacation with her in Florida. Even though she
was her best friend, she did not see how she was ever to
get her to behave properly. Susan had an absolutely un-
get-over-able idea that it was a good thing to be girlish.
She even let her hair hang loose every so often and tried
to look pretty. It spoiled everything.

Long before it was the proper time to ring the bell and
see if the porter would come to make up the berths, Susan
wanted to lie down and go to sleep. Her pain was better,
but she wanted to be lying down and sleeping.

"Aren't you going to eat anything?"

"Don't *talk* to me about food," said Susan. "You'll have
to go to the dining car. If anything comes in here and
smells like it, I'll be sick."

"Maybe that would be a good thing," said Edie. "Hood
always says, 'Once you get the load off your stomach—' "

"Shut up, do you hear?" said Susan fiercely.

They had meant to have all their meals in the compartment. They had been told to do so and to sign their names on the bill. Cousin Lyman was going to take care of it some way or other. Madam had not wanted them to have too much money on account of kidnapers or pickpockets or even just MEN, so she had arranged it. But now Edie would have to brave them all and go alone to the diner. She did not like it. Going through all the other cars to get to the diner was like traveling through an unknown, wild country—maybe Africa. They smelled of heat and oranges, and the inhabitants stared. She had a terrible time with the racketing, heaving doors. Even after she got there, she was not able to enjoy eating. There was certainly a giant kidnaper a few tables down who kept looking and looking at her. He was so big that he could see over all the other heads, and he could easily notice that she had not been in a dining car before in her life and had to be told what to do and how to write things down. It was too dark now to look out the window, so she kept her eyes on the tablecloth. The kidnaper's staring took her whole mind and made her make a bad mistake. Madam had sent her a handbag. She wasn't used to handbags, but she had had to take it.

"It's for your money and your ticket," Madam had written. "Keep your hand on it all the time."

But she had to let it rest on her lap while she ate, which she did in a hurry in order to get through before the kidnaper, and she got up in a hurry so that she could get back to the compartment and slam the door. She did not run, but she walked very fast through the African smells and slid the bolt as soon as she was inside the door. Hooray, safe! The porter had made up both berths, and Susan had climbed into the upper. There was nowhere to sit, so

Edie got into bed at once. It was then that she thought of the wonderful things she might have eaten, and all she had had was ham and eggs. It could have been "mulligatawny soup," which she had never heard of in her life, "chicken à la king," which she had just had once at the Belmont Hotel, stuffed potatoes, artichoke hearts, and "Charlotte Russe." It made her so hungry to think of them that she had to get up and search for the box of Huntley and Palmer sugar wafers Theodore had provided. She ate the whole box. Susan would be furious. They were her favorite thing, and Theodore had gotten them on that account, but she would have to try to make Susan see that people who were starving had to eat. Susan's stubbornness would have to give way for once. There were no more sugar wafers.

It was not until the next morning that she thought of the handbag, and even then not right away. She had woken up early—if you could call it being asleep to be whacked around all night by Cousin Lyman's train—and she had lain on her back and read *Frank Among the Rancheros* quietly so Susan could have her beauty sleep. After a while, a head hung upside down near the middle of her stomach.

"Good morrow, fair maiden," said the head. "How'j'you sleep?"

Edie did not answer.

"Why starest thou?" said the head.

Edie raised herself on her elbows so quickly that the book fell on the floor. She stared some more, leaning closer. The head smiled winningly from among its spots.

"You've got it," said Edie. "I can see as plain as day."

"I haven't," said Susan, drawing herself back. "It went

away in my sleep. I feel fine. How about some breakfast on this wobbling train?"

If Susan once got started on her stubbornness! Edie kept still.

"The only thing is, I'm hot," said Susan. "We must have gotten to the South already. Phew!" She threw all her bedclothes off. "I'm getting up." And her legs came over the side. Edie took a look at them.

"All right," she said. "You can have the bathroom first. And would you mind," she asked politely, "taking a look in the mirror?"

"I suppose you mean the snarls in my hair," said Susan. "That's always the trouble in my life."

She opened the door to the small toilet, and Edie could hear her yawning in front of the washstand. She did not stay there long. She came right out and tottered to Edie's bed.

"Do they *let* people have chicken pox on trains?" she said. "*I* bet it's against the law."

Edie thought it probably was, too, but she did not answer because there was a loud knock on the door.

"Quick," she said, "get back in the top berth and cover yourself up."

It was the conductor—a new conductor who had gotten on somewhere during the night—and he wanted their tickets, of course. In the middle of hunting for her handbag Edie remembered.

"I've lost them," she said suddenly.

The conductor would not believe this. He had to come into the compartment and look for himself. He looked everywhere except underneath Susan, who had rolled herself into a tight cocoon. Then he called the porter, who turned out to be a new one, too, and he looked. Edie looked herself, knowing it was hopeless. Finally, it seemed too bad to waste their time, and she told them what had happened. "It just slipped off my lap when I was eating," she said. "And I just forgot."

The porter was sent to the diner, and the conductor began asking for names.

"Look," said Edie, "my cousin is Mr. Lyman Deland. He knows about us."

The conductor did not believe this either. Edie got down on her hands and knees and felt under her bunk for the tags. She thought maybe the crack she had put them in came out on the floor.

"I cleaned out your little mess," said the porter, coming back and seeing her. "They ain't found nothin'," he said to the conductor.

Probably the kidnaper had her handbag, but you couldn't say that to the conductor. Edie looked out the window. The flat Virginia countryside was going past without a house in sight.

"I hope you won't put us off right *here*," she said.

"Hum," said the conductor, looking out himself. "Perhaps not here."

It sounded as if it might be pretty soon, though. When he had gone, Susan and she talked in whispers for a minute, asking each other if he really could do such a thing, and then sat in horrid silence.

"Even if he doesn't, I don't suppose we can get anything to eat for two days. *They* won't believe in Cousin Lyman either. If it's a new conductor and a new porter, it's probably a new dining car," said Edie.

"We've still got the sugar wafers," said Susan. "They'll keep us alive."

"No, they won't."

"Why not?"

"I ate 'em."

"Every ONE?"

Edie nodded.

The silence was still worse.

"I'm going to pray," said Susan, "but not for you."

"What I'm going to do is not get dressed. They can't put people off in their pajamas."

"I hope you'll *see* what can happen to sinners," said Susan. "And pigs!"

During the next silence and after some time, Edie was visited by a wild, wonderful thought. This thought might be God's way of protecting Susan if she had gotten in touch with Him, but Edie would have to be in on it, too. Probably God would be more Christian than Susan. Why not, she thought, lock the door, just lock the door and not open it until they got to Palm Sands? She was not sure she could keep Susan away from food for that long, but there were always the apples, and they were beginning to smell and ought to be eaten, and, if necessary, she would fight her. Susan was heavier, but Edie, on account of Theodore and Hubert, was a great deal better trained. She got off her bunk, stepped over, and slid the heavy bolt once more on the door.

"You can stop praying," she said. "I've fixed it."

"How?" said Susan.

Edie could see Susan didn't like the plan a bit, and it was chiefly on account of food. But Susan had had enough in New York to last for a week. "And when they begin banging on the door," Edie said, "you better remember it was God's idea and not go against it."

Susan looked at the door and at Edie. "I must say I didn't think He'd put things in *your* hands," she said, but gave in.

"Come on and let's play parchesi," said Edie.

They had to play in the lower bunk sitting cross-legged because they did not know how to get the top berth up, but they played and played, they drank water, ate apples, and slept, and then played some more. They waited for the conductor to come back and pound on the door, and after him they supposed a whole train crew would come and pound, but no one came except once the porter who called through and asked if they wouldn't like to have the beds made.

"No, thanks," said Edie. "We're having a rest."

It was certainly true. They had so much rest that by afternoon they were exhausted.

"Or else it's the weakness of starvation," said Susan. "I hope we won't have to be carried off the train. It would certainly scare your stepmother."

"The point is we're still on it," said Edie.

The train had been stopped for quite a while, and they abandoned their game to look longingly out of the window at the free people walking up and down a station platform. They did this until Edie saw the giant kidnaper looking square at their window. She pulled the shade down hurriedly.

"Hey," said Susan. "What did you do that for? I want to watch that dog. Did you see he had a basket in his mouth? Oh, the big, beautiful thing!"

There was a scuffle over the window shade, but Edie

managed to keep it down until the train began to move. Then she sat back on her heels.

"Oh," she said. "Oh! Susan! Widgy. How am I to go to see him? He'll die of loneliness. I don't even know if he has any water. What shall I do?"

She squeezed her hands between her knees in despair. She couldn't desert Widgy, no matter what. When she had left him in the baggage car, his nose was pressed against the grate of his traveling box. He wouldn't lie down. He had stood panting, water dripping off his tongue. The baggage man had promised to see about him, but how could you trust him to do it? She would have to go herself. She would have to risk not only the conductor, but the kidnaper. She could not desert Widgy. She began getting dressed.

"Don't let anybody in," she said.

"Suppose they nab you?"

"You go on to Palm Sands and tell Madam."

"It's not going to be very easy to do," said Susan.

One thing about Susan, though, was that she knew about animals, and she knew Edie had to go. "I don't like it right now," she said. Just the same she went to the door with Edie to let her slip quietly out.

"If I do get back, I'll give three taps," Edie said.

When she was free, out in the open part of the car, she wondered what she had been afraid of. It was light and airy after the compartment. There were a lot of respecta-ble-looking people in the parlor car seats, reading books or playing cards. Sun was coming in the windows. There was not a sign of a conductor or a kidnaper or even a porter, although she thought she saw the whisk of his white coat inside the compartment at the opposite end of

the car. She did not have far to go. There were only two
heavy doors to open. Wonderfully soon she pushed her
way through the second one into a chaos of boxes, crates,
trunks, bags, and great straw hampers. She was appalled.
This was not the way it had looked when she and Theodore left Widgy in an open corner before the train left
New York. How could she find a little dog's traveling box
in the middle of this mountain of stuff? She picked her
way around two wooden boxes as big as pianos, trying to
spy over and around it all. She climbed over some sacks
and squeezed between a pile of trunks. This let her out
into a small open place, and there, along the side of the
car, she was sure were some animal boxes. Yes! There was
Widgy's, nearest the door. Oh, joy!

A movement to her left made her raise her eyes. The
baggage man, of course. But it wasn't. It was the giant
kidnaper. He was sitting on a wooden crate that had small
round holes in it, swinging one leg. Perhaps the baggage
man was somewhere, but he wasn't *here*. She was completely alone. She dropped her eyes and for a minute forgot what she had come for. He could put her in any of
these trunks or cases, push it out the door at the next stop,
and that would be the end of her. She only forgot for an
instant. Widgy gave a little whine as if he knew she was
there. She went to his box and knelt down, but not with
her back to the kidnaper. She kept her body so that she
could see his swinging foot while she undid the latch.
Widgy was in her arms in a second, licking her face,
struggling to dance and play, but she couldn't let him. She
had to stay crouched, not even daring to shush him for
fear of breaking the spell of whatever safety there was.
How was she to get water for Widgy? She had thought

there would be something here, some arrangement to take
care of animals. She lifted the top of his box and took out
his empty water pan and then looked over the floor of the
car, not raising her eyes higher than a foot. She saw the
kidnaper's foot stop swinging, and she heard him clear his
throat.

"Can I be of any assistance?" he said.

"No, thank you," said Edie. She tried to quiet Widgy's
joy while her eyes hurried around and around the open
space.

"You and your friend seem to be having lots of trouble."

That was none of his business. How would she ever get
out of here?

"They keep the water can over there, between those
two pieces of rail, so it won't tip over."

"Thanks," said Edie. Why hadn't she seen it all the
time?

"I put your little dog near the door so he would get
some air."

"Thanks."

"You could probably let him run here a little."

It was just like a kidnaper to offer that suggestion.
Widgy would probably lift his leg on one of those green
trunks. She wasn't going to thank any kidnaper for that.
Widgy would have to behave for another day. She put his
pan carefully at one end of the box and dog biscuit at the
other and then reluctantly lifted him in. He didn't like it.
She wished she dared to stay, but it was a relief to be
almost ready to escape. She heard the kidnaper get up.

"How's your friend, the conductor?" he said in a soft,
low, grumbling voice—just the voice of a bear.

Edie fixed the latch on Widgy's box and stood up. At least *he* was all right for another day. But she had no idea now how to get away and be all right herself. All the kidnaper would have to do, now that he was standing up, was bend over and stretch out one arm. Well, at least she'd better watch him. She looked up. It was quite a way to his face, and even when her eyes got there, she did not quite see it. She saw only a lot of rough hair because she had thought of a way to put him off for a second.

"My father," she said, "does not allow me to talk to people on the train."

She did not run for the crack between the trunks that she had come in by. She took one long, slow step, slipped through, over the sacks, around the piano boxes, and out the door. Then into the sun of the next car. She was still alive! Susan let her in at once, and they bolted the door again. The next stop was Jacksonville, Florida. They were still both on the train.

"But I think I've got hunger pains," said Susan, holding her stomach.

"Try some dog biscuit," said Edie. "I stole them from Widge, but I don't think he'll mind."

No matter what Edie said or did, Susan was not going to keep the window shade down all the time while the train waited and waited at Jacksonville, Florida. In this kind of struggle, Edie did not have a chance. Susan's weight squeezed her powerlessly out of the way just by leaning on her and pushing, and then she sat on her heels simply eating up the sights outside. Edie retreated to the back of the compartment and stood with her back against the door. That fool Susan wanting to be noticed by everybody. Suppose the police were out there as well as the kidnaper? Suddenly Susan leaned forward and almost knocked her head through the glass.

"Edie," she said, "there's a man out there with a dog that's Widgy's twin. Come and look. It's exactly Widgy's twin, same markings, same size, everything. Come on and look."

Edie came forward enough to see.

"Perfectly different," she said.

"You're so conceited about Widgy that you wouldn't admit it if he *had* a twin," said Susan.

"Perfectly, absolutely different."

It was not true because that was Widgy all right and the giant kidnaper was walking away with him on a leash.

"You look awfully funny," said Susan. "You're being awfully funny the whole time. I think maybe we better get out of this hole. Maybe you're going to die or something."

"Not yet," said Edie.

It was all she was able to say. She had thought for one terrible moment that perhaps it was Widgy the kidnaper was after, but she had seen him turn and come back toward the train. Then there was another terrible moment when she could not decide whether it was all right or whether he was using her poor little dog to lure her out. She tried to remember his face, but she had not really looked at it. All she could see was his untidy curly hair.

That afternoon the porter came and knocked and knocked and talked and talked to them, but they would not answer.

"Are you dead, Misses?" he finally said.

"No," they both said together. "Go away!"

It made them laugh so much that their stomachs hurt,

and they had to hold onto them while they leaned against each other in the lower bunk. But it was the only good part of the day. The compartment smelled of apples until they wondered if they would be suffocated. They ate them all to prevent this, and then wished they hadn't. Apples made you feel hollow, they found. They drank water to fill the hollow and felt bloated. They were glad to go to bed. It was only one more day to Palm Sands, they told each other, and even if they were put off now, at least it would be warm.

In the morning, they decided that Edie should go and see Widgy early. She wanted to be sure he was there, and Susan thought some more dog biscuits would not be amiss.

"They're supposed to be made of old bones and horses' hoofs," said Edie.

"I wouldn't care if they were made of people's bones and hoofs," said Susan. "I'm beginning to shrink. Look at me." She pulled herself in all over.

It was quite a marvelous sight to see Susan getting thin right before her eyes. If she got thin enough, she would not be able to push people around just by leaning on them.

"You ought to starve more," said Edie. "You'd look twice as girlish."

"I try," said Susan meekly.

"Only when there's nothing to eat," said Edie severely, but you really had to give in to Susan when she was meek. "You're very good-looking, anyway," she added with a grin.

This time when they opened the door it was so early that the sleeping berths outside were not folded up, and

Edie passed them between two lines of long green cur-
tains. The car smelled of snoring people, and she could
even hear one or two. She hurried out the door at the
other end.

The baggage car was just as full as it had been, but the
baggage was different. Only the space in the middle was
the same. And no one was there. Bliss unconfined, just like
a hymn. *No one*. Edie had a good time comforting Widgy,
letting him run, making him jump for dog biscuits and
stand swaying on the trunks while the train lurched. It
looked so much fun that she tried it herself, jumping from
one trunk to another, to a crate, to a box—gee, there were
the kidnaper's big boxes, still there, with their little holes,
but probably he was asleep—to a mountain of boxes and,
taking a leap, landed exactly right and then tried another.
The spaces between were chasms; at the bottom, a river
boiled and foamed over rocks. If she missed, it would
drown her in a second. She did not miss, not once, and
Widgy tore after her barking as if he were crazy, but on
her last jump she started a kind of avalanche—not much
—just enough to have one big trunk land on the corner of
one of the kidnaper's boxes and tip it over. She didn't see
that it did any harm, and as she was now awfully hot—
they must be nearly to Palm Sands—she decided she had
better go back. After putting Widgy in his case, she filled
her pockets with dog biscuits. She felt like Susan at this
point. No matter what they were made of, she would be
glad to eat them. As she passed the kidnaper's box, she
looked at it apologetically. It was a very strong box,
locked up with a strong iron latch. That trunk must have
been full of bricks because it had loosened one of the
boards. She felt more apologetic, particularly if the kid-

naper was keeping a tiger in there; it had been turned
upside down. It might want to get out. Whatever it was
was trying. As the loose board gave a jerk up, Edie
thought she saw a nose. Of course, a nose was nothing. No
animal would really get through that crack, but she kept
her eyes on it. She would so much like to know what kind
of animal it was. Before she had time to take another
breath, she knew. A flat beady-eyed head came out, pulling the rest of itself after it little by little. By the time
the whole of it flopped on the floor like a big coil of
rope, she was out of the car. She knew it was a terrible
thing, but she did not have time to close that heavy door.
She had to get to the next one. This she did struggle to
close, and the porter came to help her, but the snake's
head got through first, and when he saw it, the porter
said, "Oh, my Christians Anderson," let go the door, and
began to back up. Edie was sure this was the wrong thing
to do. Instead, she slipped sideways into an empty seat,
pulled up her legs, and looked out the window. Perhaps
she hadn't seen any snake. There was a rustle going
through the car, but perhaps that was just— She had to
edge over toward the aisle and look. The snake was there,
all right, sliding along with the porter in front of it, and
every person in the car leaning over to see what they
could see. There were only backs of heads; no one was
saying a word. She leaned, too, saw the porter reach the
door, get through, and pull it to behind him. The snake
almost bumped its nose on it and then waved its head
around, looking for some place to go. "Oh, my Christians
Anderson," Edie thought. "Suppose it comes back!" It did
something worse. It slithered slowly, but certainly, into
their own compartment. That terrible Susan, she must

have opened the door! How could she have done it against
all orders! She deserved a snake! She deserved a family of
snakes! Let them bite her! Edie got to her wobbly legs.
After all, she had let the snake out. She would never forgive Susan for being an obstinate donkey and opening the
door, but she would have to try to rescue her. All the
heads turned to look at her as she went past, and somebody tried to catch her dress and say something, but she
twitched away. At the compartment door she stopped.
Her legs wouldn't take her in, even though the snake was
not in sight. She had to steady herself with a hand on
either side.

"Hey," she said in a croak.

"Hey," said Susan cheerfully from the top berth. "You
know what's happened?"

"Yes," said Edie, "there's a big snake in here. He just
came through the door."

"You're mad, I suppose, because I left it open. But it's
all right. We're free. We can have breakfast. I was just
waiting for you. I'll tell you about it."

"Susan," said Edie, "stay there. *Don't* get down. You'll
step on him."

"You can't scare me," said Susan. "I'm hungry, and my
spots are almost gone. It was a light case for fair."

She swung her legs over the side of the berth.

How could you rescue a person like Susan? She was like
a wild steamroller that just went on regardless, squashing
objections and taking her own way. Her dangling white
legs would be just the thing any snake would bite as soon
as it saw them. It was just luck that, when she looked
down to see where to jump, she saw the snake first. It had

gone under the compartment chair and now came out to get to the darkness under the lower berth.

"Wheee," said Susan. "I guess you're right."

This was the last conversation they had together for some time. Suddenly there was such a noise behind Edie that she turned to face it. Everyone in the car seemed to be there crowding and pushing, trying to see what was happening to Susan and her. She was shoved into the middle of the room.

"Get back," she said furiously. "You get back out of here and let us get out."

No one moved at all; they just shoved some more, and Edie was pushed nearer the bunk. She would have to jump into it or up where Susan was, or do something, somehow. It was no use yelling at them; they were all making so much noise themselves that they wouldn't hear. She thought of turning and pounding at them with her fists. But suddenly there was even more noise, a regular roar at the back of the crowd. All the people seemed to be sucked away from the door by it, and still roaring (and it sounded like swearing), the giant kidnaper paddled people away like a swimmer and came out in front of them.

"*Where?*" he said.

Edie pointed. She had stepped back herself.

It took him only two seconds to catch that snake. He gathered up the dragging bedclothes, hurled them on top of Susan, tipped up the top berth with her in it, and, crouching, with two easy, quick movements of his hands, had the snake by the head and tail, stretched out and helpless. The crowd cheered slightly. It was probably not as much fun as seeing Susan bitten, but they must have been somewhat relieved. In the end, the snake could have come out and got them. To Edie, it seemed an awfully brave thing to have done, until the kidnaper said: "It's a young boa constrictor, ladies and gentlemen, nothing to be afraid of. Boa constrictors don't bite. They squeeze their prey." The kidnaper wouldn't have minded if his snake had squeezed that whole crowd; that was easy to see. "But this one is too young," he said. "You have managed to give me a bad scare." He walked through the crowd holding the snake like a lance in front of him. No one wanted to be squeezed instead of bitten, so they gave him room. Edie and Susan were left alone.

"What a noble-looking man," said Susan. "He saved our lives."

Edie would not talk about the giant kidnaper. She didn't know *what* he was. She listened instead to Susan's story about how, while she was away, a man had held up a sign outside the window at one of the train stops. It had said: "Attention, young ladies. Your unkle done wire."

After that, of course, as soon as she could stop giggling, Susan had opened the door and ordered breakfast. "Two of everything," she said, "and it ought to be here any minute."

Cousin Lyman's wire changed them in a twinkle from orphans to princesses, and they felt they might as well enjoy it. Edie asked for chicken à la king for Widgy, and Susan requested a third order of pancakes. She also interviewed the porter about that noble-looking man with the snake. Of all inquisitive people, Susan was the worst! But the porter hardly knew a thing about him. All he knew was that "Mr. Tom was the dangdest—travelin' up and down this Coast Line Road with his snakes." The porter was much more interested in himself.

"I thought I was done for," he said.

He tidied and cleaned and put everything straight. He even got clean white towels for them to sit on. "Who let that snake go prowlin' out," he said to himself. "Mr. Tom, he too careful."

Edie and Susan looked out the window and didn't answer, and he was gone with his suspicions when they turned around. It had all been a close shave, but now they could be comfortable. In the middle of the morning, because it was getting very warm, they changed into summer dresses and felt so comfortable that Susan wanted to go to the diner for lunch.

"You haven't any handbag to lose any more, so it's perfectly safe," she said.

Edie wasn't entirely sure. The kidnaper was still on the train, and probably he knew as well as the porter exactly who had let his snake go prowling around. She could not mention that, so she tried something else. Susan's spots were much dimmer, but they were still there.

"People will think you're covered with pimples," she said.

It made no impression. "Let 'em," said Susan. "I want to see a dining car."

There were two empty seats all ready for them in the diner, and they were shown into them by the head waiter with hand wavings and bowings, all on account of Cousin Lyman and his telegram. Of course Cousin Lyman couldn't know that there was the kidnaper two tables down staring as usual with all his might. He had probably been lying in wait. It couldn't be an accident that he was always around. He must have arranged it. Edie started to back up, but Susan was behind her and bumped her along.

"There's that noble-looking snake man," she whispered. "Good luck for us."

A lot she knew. Well, they would be in Palm Sands now in a few minutes—in about a hundred and twenty minutes —and Madam would meet them, and then the kidnaper would have to get off their trail. In the meantime, she would keep her eyes on the tablecloth and the food. But whoever could have a chance of doing the right thing with Susan around? "Did you see what he was *eating*," she said. "Two steaks, and at least seven vegetables. He must be an ogre."

"Well, if he's that," said Edie, "I wouldn't pay any attention to him if I were you."

It was a very lucky thing, she thought, that food could almost always take Susan's attention off *any*thing. Particularly today, when she had two days to make up. Otherwise, she would surely have tried to become a southern belle for the kidnaper. She had started already by flinging her braid over her shoulder by the time the soup came. She had another chance while he was eating his mountains and mountains of ice cream. In fact, she had a lot of chances because, although they got back to their compartment safely, it was not just one hundred and twenty minutes more to Palm Sands, or anything like it. Cousin Lyman's train was seven hours late. When it did finally and slowly jolt to a last stop, it was eleven o'clock at night, very dark, and as far as they could see, right in the middle of a Florida jungle. There were lots of people there, crowding under some globe lights, but no one for them, and they had to ask the porter if they were really in Palm Sands. "Sure is," he said. "Any more there, we'd be in the sea."

They could see it themselves, glimmering beyond some palm trees.

Of course, right then up came the kidnaper. Of course, this was his chance and, of course, Susan welcomed him like a long lost friend. She explained everything. She told him who they were and what Madam's address was and why they were there.

"We're terribly sorry we let out your snake," she said finally. "But will you please help us?"

All Edie could do was pretend she didn't hear a thing. She did not hear Susan going on and on, nor the kidnaper whistle for what turned out to be a wheelchair boy, nor the directions given, nor the kidnaper's last remark. "Good night, girls. When you get home, tell your father there's another father in the world."

As they were pushed along in the chair, which seemed like a huge wicker basket, she did hear Susan say: "What did I tell you? He's a noble man."

But Edie wasn't going to listen to her. She had managed to get her to Palm Sands in spite of all her foolishnesses, and she'd better be a little more thankful. Edie put her head back against the wheelchair and drew in her breath. "This is the best smelling place I ever was in," she said.

Five

+-+- ❀ -+-+

THE MIRACLES

The best room in Madam's house in Palm Sands was for Susan because she was a guest, so she had the one looking out on the beach and the ocean. Edie's was at the back and looked out only on those yellow globes that Palm Sands used to light its paths and streets. There were not many of them. It must be a little place. This was all she had time to think before she flopped into bed the first night. When she woke up the next morning, it was raining. In fact, every morning during the whole vacation, before she opened her eyes, she heard the rain. She even smelled it and felt it. The first morning it had made her sad; no swimming, no bikes, no sand. What would they do? In Florida there was supposed to be sun all the time. This wasn't fair. She had turned away from the window and tried to make it stop, but there it still was in her ears, a soft separated patter.

Every morning, the whole vacation, when Edie opened her eyes, it wasn't raining at all. The sun was glancing over everything as if it were being scattered from bags of light, and rustling palm fronds were making the sound of rain.

This was the way Florida turned out to be, miracles happening any time. Even Widgy had had one practiced on him. It was not a good one, and he didn't like it, but he would have had to admit he would never have believed it could happen. Jippy, Madam's fox terrier, who was as meek as a mole at home, bit him on the ear the minute he came through the screen door. Everything was a surprise, like the palm fronds, with their rain sounds.

She and Susan had not much wanted to come here after the ice storm. They had wanted to see what would happen next. They had thought that if everybody else went to stay with Madam and left them in Summerton, it would be nice for her and nice for them, too.

No one else was in favor of it, however. Cook and Gander were enjoying their vacation, and Theodore gave his opinion that it would be better to keep those two kids where they could be seen, as he said, "with the naked eye."

They had been a little against Palm Sands when they started out. Edie thought they might have to change their clothes ten or twelve times a day, and although Susan said they couldn't because they didn't have that many, she was prejudiced on account of "the rich." The rich in Palm Sands, she had heard, were particularly sinful, and she asked Edie to remember about the Bible saying that you could not touch pitch "without being defiled."

"The trouble with you is, you get all your ideas from ministers," said Edie. "We're not going to *touch* anybody. Maybe you've heard that a cat can look at a king even if it

isn't in the Bible." Edie asked her to remember that the
good died young.

They took their prejudices to the very door of Madam's
house and kept them while Widgy was being bitten. The
next morning, the prejudices vanished. It was because of
Edie's experience about the rain.

"Miracles are only in the Bible," she said. "So Palm
Sands must be a very good place, to have them happen
here."

If Susan was still doubtful, she had to give in right
away. When they got to the top of the stairs on their way
down to breakfast, they heard a man's voice in the hall
below—a soft, grumbling voice. It was the only voice like
that in the world. The kidnaper! In this house, talking to
Madam! Standing there in front of her with his head covered with curls and his eyebrows tipped up like the devil's, Susan's wonderful man was nothing but a great big
baby, taking a scolding. If that wasn't a miracle—to
meet him in this house and find him so different from a
villain!

They listened to him, delighted, and to Madam answering.

"No, Tom," she said, "if you want to stay, you'll have to
keep your snakes out of the bathtub and use it yourself."

He kept right on grumbling. The Indian he usually left
his snakes with had gone fishing, his boat didn't leave for
Guatemala for two days, and he had had a bath at the
hotel the night before.

Edie thought they should go down and help Madam
out. She was sure she didn't want snakes in the house
either.

"This is Mr. Barlow, the naturalist, girls, and an old friend of mine," Madam said.

Mr. Barlow made them a sort of distant bow. "Your stepdaughter, Mrs. Cares," he said, "is not a friendly person."

To make up for Edie's rudeness, he was allowed to stay in the downstairs guest room if he kept the bathroom door locked and did not mention a snake of any kind inside the house. If the servants ever heard what kind of visitors Madam had, they would be on the first train back to New York.

"My dear lady," said Mr. Barlow, "I bow to all your commands and will execute them faithfully."

He padded with his cat steps to the front door and was back with a bag before you could say Jack Robinson. The snakes had been on the piazza all the time!

"I bet you never lived with a boa constrictor before," Edie said to Susan later. Susan was really impressed with what Palm Sands could provide, no matter how sinful it was.

The third miracle was Palm Sands itself, starting with Madam's house, Spray Cottage. It was just a house, and except for the bedroom and sitting room where Madam kept her own things, there was nothing in it. There was a large free hall with rooms on either side, and upstairs just the same. There were chairs, naturally, and beds, and places to put clothes, but it was all so empty something else got in—the smell of straw matting, wood smoke, and sea. Nothing interfered with this. Food smells blew out the back door, Edie supposed, because in Florida doors and windows were open all the time. Sun came in, too, but by afternoon a breeze came after it and somehow or other swept it shady. There might have been almost too much sun in Florida if it had not been for this breeze and the palm trees. Like the yellow globes Palm Sands used at night to light its streets, the palm trees took care of it in the daytime. They broke up the light. They lined the streets, stood on lawns, and when there were free spaces, leaned this way and that in clusters. What was left was jungle. Edie and Susan meant to investigate this, too, but kept putting it off in order to ride the bikes Madam had gotten for them through the alleys and down the lanes of leaning, curving palms.

"The palms, the palms, the palms," Edie sang at the top of her voice along the Lake Path.

"It's like the South Seas on a postcard," said Susan, coming up with her.

"I think it's like the Garden of Eden," said Edie, "and you couldn't put that on a postcard."

The drawback at first to all their expeditions was that Widgy couldn't come. Palm Sands might be the Garden of Eden, but there were automobiles in it, just the same, and every so often the bicycle paths went across their roads. Widgy was a good dog and would do almost anything Edie asked him to, but he would not go last when they were bicycling. He had to go first, and particularly at crossroads, to see what smells were on the other side. Several people in autos had said loud things at them, and one man got out and shook his fist. They stuck out their tongues at him, but it didn't calm him down, and he said that the next time he would run over their "—— dog." So they had to leave Widgy at home. He did not like it, and neither did Madam when he climbed on the chintz-covered sofa top to look out the window for them, or skithered up the straw matting when he thought they were coming. Madam thought of a bicycle basket. From then on he sat up on front of Edie's bike, his hair and whiskers blowing backwards, watching all the sights with great interest.

They used their bicycles like ponies. For Palm Sands they were better than ponies. They didn't have to be groomed or fed and could go anywhere, and Palm Sands, as Edie had thought, was a little place. It had a drugstore, a post office, and a store to buy writing paper. No more village than that. *Its* miracle was that it had other things they never would have believed.

"For instance, the Marble Palace," said Edie.

They found it not long after they came, in a kind of jungle place that looked as if God had started to make a world there and then got tired and not finished it. There were long marble-paved drives that led to nowhere except the lake that was opposite the Palm Sands ocean. Most of the drives were cracked and uneven, but the one leading to the Marble Palace was perfect. And the palace itself was perfect: old, deserted, stained green with moss, but made of marble and enormous, which was the right size for it to be. They rode up and down and around and around on the flat marble, making guesses about the palace and who could own such a marvelous place and not live in it.

"Except they do cut the jungle," Susan noticed.

That was true. The jungle was kept back. But nothing ever happened there. It forced them to explore farther and wider, and they found that Palm Sands seemed to have been arranged especially so they could enjoy it. At least nowhere else that they had ever heard of would they have been able to use other people's property so easily. There were no fences and, of course, no stone walls. Sometimes there were gates, but they stood bare and alone to mark a drive that ran deep into trees and shrubs, and they had no wire or rails attached to them.

"It gets more and more like the Kingdom of Heaven," said Susan.

"It's the rich," said Edie slyly.

She made Susan admit that it didn't matter whether people were rich or not as long as they didn't care who came around and used their things. They discovered a zoo one full moonlight night after Madam had gone upstairs to bed. The best thing about bikes was that they made no noise, and all they had to do about Widgy was put down the cover on his basket. They got to the zoo by following the smell of orange blossoms. The idea came to them both at the first whiff as they were riding along the Ocean Boulevard to enjoy the moon. They slowed their bikes, and when the smell turned down a drive they turned, too, coasted down a slope, and there they were in an orange grove, suddenly right in the middle of it. They found they were in the middle of a zoo as well when they kept hearing rustlings and noises. It wasn't a public zoo. It belonged to someone, obviously, but to what kind of person they couldn't imagine.

"Cages!" said Edie.

"Oh, the poor things!"

But the animals seemed quite comfortable and were not disturbed by being looked at in the moonlight.

There was one animal that was free, and this was a spider monkey. He had a house in a tree, and they only

saw him because he opened his door and came out to take
a look at them. Edie remarked that it was still more like
the Garden of Eden.

"I hope there aren't any serpents," Susan said, looking
into the darkness under the orange trees.

"They're all at our house," said Edie. It made Susan
giggle, and the giggle brought the monkey down from his
tree.

Without even a good look at her, that monkey loved
Susan. He did look at Edie and bared his teeth at her,
chattering. So he was Susan's monkey, and she made the
rules about him. Edie would have liked to bring him
crackers and nuts to make friends.

"You don't feed animals you don't know about *anything*," said Susan.

Edie always had to empty her pockets before they visited the zoo.

"How do *you* know he *is* a spider monkey?"

"There's a sign on the tree. Yah to you," said Susan.

Edie thought they ought to tell somebody the monkey
was loose.

"Not while he behaves."

He did behave. He tried to hide things in Susan's hair,
and he wanted to hug her too many times, and he made
angry noises when they wandered around the zoo cages,
looking at foxes and lynxes and ocelots, but not at the
snakes.

"Ugh! We've seen enough of those," Edie said.

The monkey tried to snatch at the animals in the cages,
but always, when the girls left, he got down slowly from
Susan's shoulder and sat in the middle of the lane with his
hands to his mouth. He did not try to follow them. The

way he looked made Susan go back and tell him she
would come again. It almost upset his behavior. He would
take a few running steps on all fours.

"Be good," Susan would say sternly.

So he would stop and sit down again.

Susan was rather ridiculous about her old monkey. She
wanted to spend all the time of the full moon with him.
Edie had to lure her away by saying she knew another
path to explore. She pumped her bicycle up the little zoo
hill, one night, calling her rallying cry in a whisper, "The
palms, the palms, the palms." Susan had to come. The
rallying cry was magic and had to be obeyed.

The other drive came out on a lawn where there was a
tennis court with some humps beside it. This time they
had to be more careful. There were some lights on in the
house above them.

"Whiz, people living here," said Edie. "What are *those*
things?"

Although they thought they had made no noise, one of
the humps got up and stood listening. Drawing back, Edie
hit a bush, and all the humps began to get up and listen.
They all looked alike, and their heads were the shape of
croquet mallets.

"Whiz, it's those birds Alice played croquet with. Whiz,
whiz, it's a flock of flamingos!"

They retreated, inch by inch, hoping the flamingos
would forget them and, as they stepped from the bushes
on the other side forgot the flamingos and even the lighted
house because of what they now saw before them beside
the moon-drenched tennis court. Someone had forgotten
to take in the tea things! There was a pitcher half full of
iced tea, another of lemonade, a pile of sandwiches, and a

coconut cake with its fringes curled and shining, hardly eaten at all.

They took just enough time, after they had finished, to lick their fingers and wipe them on the lawn grass and then silently stole away. They never went back to this paradise. There were the lighted windows, of course, but they were too awed by their own good luck. It could not be the same again, ever, they agreed, and were a little sad to think that never again in all their lives would they find a feast set out for them in moonlight.

They found one more paradise, and this they went to, often. It was not as grand as the others, but it had one grand thing—a swimming pool in an arcade of white pillars. At first they were afraid. It was very near the house. Great white steps led up from it to the house's terrace. But as the moon got smaller and later, they felt safer and bolder. The people, if there were any, never went out at night—anyway, not to use their swimming pool.

They thought they might as well use it instead. They swam every morning in the ocean, naturally, but slipping at night into black water, as if they were seals, and floating, with the arcade rising around and above them, made them feel as if they were on the moon itself, rocked in the black sky. One night after the moon had gone they felt completely safe and were floating, cool and content, admiring the Florida stars, when—dreadfully—the pool, the arcade, and even part of the shrubbery were lighted from end to end, every nook and cranny, every inch of water! It was just another miracle that they were able to climb out and pelt into the jungle, grabbing up their clothes as they went. Once there, in the thick dark, if fifty gardeners and a hundred owners had been after them, they could not have moved. They had crashed into vines and clinging things that held them immovable. They heard people come out, talking and laughing, who looked at the pool and arcade and then went in again. When the lights finally were turned out, they had to pick vines and leaves off their arms and legs and crawl out on their stomachs to get free. They dressed like lightning.

"It's lucky those people are so foolish," said Edie. "If they weren't, we'd probably be on the way to jail."

Susan had been badly scared.

"It would have been an awful surprise to your stepmother," she said. "I don't believe she knows what we're doing."

"That's the luckiest thing of all," said Edie virtuously. "Because if she got worried and had asthma, we'd have to stop."

They talked things over the next morning as they lay on the beach and decided they had better stop, anyway. Palm Sands people were beginning to use their own property. It was awfully mean of them, but they supposed they had a right. They put their bicycles away for a few days and wandered about disconsolate with Chris and Lou, hunting shells and looking for places where turtles might have laid their eggs. Mr. Barlow had said there were such places, but they never found any. Life was boring and beyond all hope. They kept thinking of Summerton and the ponies.

"We never had to stop using *them*," said Edie.

"They never got us into trouble," said Susan.

But after all Palm Sands did not go back on them. Strolling home from the drugstore one afternoon, they stopped on the path that led past the Coconut Grove, an outdoor restaurant, and watched people having tea and dancing. They were not allowed to go in, but even from outside the ropes, they could see quite well, well enough so that while they were looking—at that very exact moment—they saw a coconut fall out of a tree and land bang in the middle of one of the tin tables. Everything jumped, glasses, bottles, cups, spoons, sandwiches; they watched them go up like tennis balls, and a lady in a big hat, trying to get out of the way, went over backwards with her feet and her petticoats in the air. They rocked home holding their stomachs and leaning against palm trees.

"Oh dear, oh don't, oh dear, oh don't," was all they could say to each other.

Then the next day Madam asked them to go with her to tea at the Hotel. After that they had the Hotel. They had not noticed it before.

When they did notice it, they saw that it was like the other houses in Palm Sands, but bigger, much bigger. In fact, they were never able to think of any building as big as the Hotel. It spread itself in front of the ocean like a one-roofed town, on and on, and when it came to a stop, its piazzas began, broad and endless—everything, every last part of it, made of good-smelling, sun-baked wood. It was painted white, but the smell somehow got through the paint not only outside but also inside, where it was white, too, with green carpets and green shrubs around. The halls, the wonderful, marvelous halls as wide as roads, were carpeted with red. They weren't sure if it was because of the color or because the halls were so wide that they had to run down them. They couldn't help themselves.

In the afternoons when the Hotel seemed to be abandoned by all its customers, they made its corridors their race track. They raced pell-mell through all four floors, back and forth, spurning the red carpet beneath their sneakers, taking the stairs like flying fish, and finally flinging themselves out the great back door that faced the sea to lie on the grass plot, panting themselves strong again.

They loved the Hotel.

Naturally, when they were in it with Madam, they had to act like what Hood called "civilized beings," but "civilized beings," they found, could have glasses of iced orangeade with sliced pineapple and cherries, could look in shop windows at diamonds, pearls, rubies, emeralds, and gold, could stare at whole roomsful of fruit done up in paper and ribbons, nuts in silver baskets, chocolate creams in crimson foil, and ONE big room of flowers— just flowers. The smell of each one came out a little into the corridor, especially the flowers. Especially Parma violets. The women they met who happened to wear them in a bunch at their waists they edged away from, frowning. It was a sin to wear Parma violets and let them die of thirst.

When they discovered that the Hotel did not mind dogs and that Widgy could have as much fun as themselves on the race track, they spent almost every afternoon there. Conveniently, its corridors had extra doors, and there was no need to go past the desk opposite the grand staircase. Widgy could come trotting in behind them, meek and obedient, at the door facing the sea. He seemed to know just what to do, climbing the stairs on the carpet and not making a sound. When they started their race, he raced with them, skithering ahead and always winning. It made him almost crazy with joy. They patted him and petted him for being so good and so silent.

"We praised him too much," said Susan later. "It went to his head."

But Edie would not go back on Widgy. She was sure he had smelled the manager coming—probably from a long way away. Anyhow, in the middle of a run with Widgy, who for the first time had started barking like a twenty-two rifle, the manager suddenly was there in front of them, and if they had not separated like lightning, they would have butted him down flat. Instead, he was able to catch an arm of each one, and although he staggered back, he did not let go. He was quite big, and he was quite red in the face. He shook them as if they were dead rabbits.

"Out," he said, pointing to the back door. "OUT."

They went, tiptoeing, quickly, and so did Widgy, dancing around them still barking. The manager had to shout.

"*Do not come back!*" he said.

Losing the Hotel, Edie and Susan told each other, was the most miserable thing that had ever happened to them. It was worse than the loss of all the other paradises put together. Somehow it had made them feel as fleet as deer and as strong as elephants to have the air fly backwards in the breeze of the corridors. There was nothing that could make up for it. When Mr. Barlow came back from Guatemala, they tried to be interested in him.

They found him on the porch of Spray Cottage one afternoon smoking a cigar as big as a water pipe.

"The Madam has put me out," he said. "Can't stand the smell of cigars."

"I love cigars," said Susan, tossing back her braid. But she gave a squeak and a hop when she found she was standing beside a canvas bag that was by his chair.

"Bones," he said. "Your stepmother," he said, "has turned ugly about snakes."

"Bones!" Susan said. "Why? For the dogs or something?"

"No, you little ignoramus," Mr. Barlow replied cordially, blowing smoke. "Old bones. Ancient bones. Thousand-year-old ones. Million-year-old ones. Because they interest me."

"They wouldn't interest the dogs," Edie said.

He was to stay with them until the rest of the family came, three days before Christmas, on condition that he keep the bones in the back yard. Madam had a lot of conditions about Mr. Barlow. He couldn't wear bare feet in the house. They heard her say: "Tom, I don't want your dreadful toes under my table when I eat."

Mr. Barlow perked Edie and Susan up a little. He was really quite interesting. He lived with a frog, for one thing. When he went away, his wife had to live with it alone and write down everything it did. She would not go on trips with it because of having to catch flies in hotels for its meals. For another thing, Mr. Barlow believed in ghosts. Madam made another rule about that. He was not to bring any of his ghosts into her house.

"They wouldn't come," said Mr. Barlow. "Their manners are better than some people's."

"No, Tom," said Madam. "I forbid it."

With their teeth chattering in fright, Edie and Susan got together one night and implored one of Mr. Barlow's ghosts to appear in Susan's room. It wouldn't, although when the wind tapped the window, Susan had leaped into bed and covered her head with the blanket.

"If you think that's good manners," said Edie.

Still, no matter how interesting, you couldn't sit around all day listening to grown people talk. It made your bones ache. For life to be any good, something had to happen or you had to do something. They could not really hope for another falling coconut; indeed, they had been sorry to see that the day after that one had fallen, there were men on ladders all over Palm Sands knocking coconuts down for fear somebody would be brained by one. So when Mr. Barlow asked them to go alligator hunting, they jumped at the chance. They did not know how to hunt alligators. It was something they had never thought of at all, but what they did know was that something was better than nothing. Things in Palm Sands were changing and becoming frightful. They had not only lost their paradises and the Hotel, but they were also losing the whole of Palm Sands. The palm paths were getting full of other people; at the drugstore they had to wait for their sodas behind the backs of a lot of older boys and girls who had come from they didn't know where—they were hardly able to *get* sodas. These talkers and laughers seemed so much to think they owned the place. The golf course was covered with fat men smoking cigars who didn't want anyone near it. As for Widgy, one fat man took a swipe at him with a golf club. They had to leave Widgy at home. He couldn't understand either why everything had suddenly changed. He was nearly run over right in front of Spray Cottage by a bunch of bicyclists who were chattering so hard that they couldn't look where they were going. All miracles had ceased. They refused to happen in crowds. So when

Mr. Barlow said Widgy could come hunting, too, it seemed exactly the right thing to do, and they thought Mr. Barlow not only interesting but also kind. Edie was extremely sorry that she had ever imagined him to be a kidnaper.

Mr. Barlow was allowed to use Madam's Ford to take them to the Everglades if he promised to leave it in plain sight. He had borrowed it once before and the next morning couldn't remember what he had done with it. Edie and Susan had been sent out on their bicycles to search the whole of Palm Sands while Mr. Barlow tried to pacify Madam. They had found the car, looking lost and innocent, on a back street outside the place belonging to an Indian who sold skins.

There was nothing in the Everglades at all except swamp, and the Ford could be seen for miles, so there was no difficulty about that. Alligator hunting turned out to be walking along in a muddy brook with a stick. Mr. Barlow said to thump the stick in front of them and, if it came down on top of an alligator, to let him know.

"You'll have to look alive," he said.

"How big will these alligators be?" said Susan, going very slowly and thumping like anything.

Edie couldn't answer. She was doing the same and, besides, was thinking about boa constrictors, copperheads, rattlesnakes, and how if she were an alligator and anyone came down on her head with a stick, she would certainly make an awful fuss whether she was big or little.

"I suppose they all have the same kind of teeth," she said, which was what Susan certainly wanted to know.

"I've read," said Susan, "that an alligator can flip you into its mouth with its tail."

Conversing like this made them very slow, and it annoyed Mr. Barlow.

"We'll get no 'gators at this rate," he called to them, trying to urge them on.

"We've been thinking they might get us," Susan called back.

"Pshaw!" said Mr. Barlow. "Stir your stumps!"

He could certainly say some very cruel things. It might have been better if he had stayed a kidnaper. By now Father would have paid the ransom, and they would be safe home, waiting for Christmas. Now they would probably be bitten and die. Mr. Barlow would put their bones in a bag and keep them in the back yard. Edie was furious. When she did come down on an alligator, she hit him so hard that she had time to fall flat on her face on the bank before he lashed at her. It was a very small 'gator, Mr. Barlow said grumbling, hardly worth taking, so he threw him back downstream—where he could get Edie on the way home—and nearly on top of Widgy, who had to give a hop to get out of the way. Widgy was not enjoying it either. He walked on the bank as if he were on pins and needles. Poor Widge! Whatever the Everglades was covered with hurt his feet. And now the alligator was in it, he had to stay out of the brook.

Susan had stayed glued to her spot in the brook, watching the alligator fly through the air and splash down again.

"Get busy," said Mr. Barlow heartlessly.

They worked themselves along like two pilgrims who had peas in their shoes and had lost their faith. They hardly noticed Mr. Barlow when he stepped out of the brook onto a sort of island and sat down on a tree stump.

"Lunch," he called.

They all sat on stumps to eat what Madam's cook had put up for them—chicken sandwiches with tomato and mayonnaise, with Lady Baltimore cake for dessert. It was a good lunch all right, but even Susan seemed to be less enthusiastic than usual. The sun in Florida practically never set, and they would be thumping for alligators, if they did not die sooner, forever and ever.

"I never saw so much of nothing," said Susan sadly, looking at the Everglades.

"That's a very ignorant remark," said Mr. Barlow. He had a sandwich in each hand and took bites out of them in turn. They had forgotten he was an ogre, though Madam had had to make a rule about what he ate, too. They were a little deaf to what he was saying, but it didn't stop him from explaining.

"It is ignorant because that out there"—he waved a great hand—"is teeming with life. Life that's alive and life that's dead. See that smoke over there?" He pointed a sandwich at the horizon. "Indians."

"You mean with feathers and tomahawks!" said Susan, gaping.

Edie knew exactly what she was thinking. Now they were going to be scalped!

This did not seem to matter to Mr. Barlow. "Well, Indians," he said. "And everywhere alligators, birds, snakes, otters, deer, aboveground, and underground many more— elephants, three-toed horses, camels, rhinoceros, tigers, antelopes, sloths, mastodons." He lifted his hands. "Garden of Eden," he said.

It was certainly different from what they had thought!

"I never heard about a single alligator in the Garden of

Eden, did you?" said Susan in a whisper as they started back to their brook.

"Maybe God invented them later," said Edie.

Anyway, they were here. Hadn't they seen one!

They thumped and thumped with the sun blazing down until Edie found the channel half dammed up by an old bleached piece of wood. She tried to go around it, but when she put her foot on the bank, she found the swamp had turned so marshy that her whole foot disappeared. She had to dig for her sneaker, and it tired her out. She sat down on the wood to rest. Her fingers felt for a piece of bark to keep Widgy amused so he would not try to get muddily into her lap, but the bark wouldn't come off. She looked down at what she was sitting on. It wasn't wood at all. It wasn't rock. Thank heavens it wasn't alive! It was . . .

"Hey!" she called to Susan. "I think I've found a bone! A great big one! Maybe a mastodon."

Mr. Barlow whirled around as though stung by a bee.

"Bone?" he shouted. "Mastodon?" And he came leaping squelchily through the marsh.

But Susan squelched over first and looked with pleasure at the bone.

"Thank the good Lord," she said. "Now we can give up alligators."

The next day, Mr. Barlow and the mastodon hip bone disappeared. They had to. Edie had to leave the sound of rain and go into Susan's room to the sound of the sea. The Littles had to go to the Hotel with Hood. That just left room in Spray Cottage for Father, Theodore, Hubert, and Jane, who were all coming on an afternoon train for

Christmas. Edie and Susan were sent to meet them. They went reluctantly, like two snails, crawling along, and hitting trees with their hands in order to waste time. This was the final invasion. Even Spray Cottage would belong to the enemy. It would prevent anything happening for years.

"Well, it's always darkest before daylight," said Susan, trying to be encouraging.

Edie did not even answer.

The station was just below the Hotel. It wasn't much of a station—just a group of palm trees and a little house where a man, who got off baggage and answered questions if he happened to be there, usually sat. The train today, he said, was several hours late, as usual.

"That's good," said Edie. "Let's get a soda."

They dawdled to the drugstore and dawdled back along the path that led from the lake to the sea. They would go home and go swimming again, but just now they felt so full and tired that Edie suggested they lie down on the edge of the golf course. No one was on it now. In fact, just as always, there was no one at all around Palm Sands at three o'clock in the afternoon. They had never been able to decide where people went—perhaps to each other's houses to eat lunch. Anyway, they were never where they could be seen. Edie and Susan stretched out, patting their stomachs, with their faces to the sky.

"We can't stay here for 'several hours,'" Susan said.

"We'll just have a little rest," said Edie.

She closed her eyes against the glare.

When she opened them again, there was a vulture circling just above them. Maybe he thought they were dead. She watched his circles getting wider and wider until he was passing over the Hotel. Oh, the dear Hotel! How terrible it was that they could never go back to it! The vulture must be looking right down one of its chimneys. Then she saw something she did not believe. If she had seen the moon dropping out of the sky, she wouldn't have believed it either. It couldn't happen; it was *against* what could happen. She shut her eyes and opened them. It hadn't gone away.

"Susan," she said, "wake up and look at the Hotel chimney."

"Don't be a pest," said Susan.

"You do it!"

Susan rolled over and looked up with one eye.

"Look beside it. Do you see it?"

"Yes," said Susan.

They waited for the world to blow up. Nothing happened. No one was paying attention. There was not a stir or a sound in the lazy Palm Sands afternoon. No matter what the manager had said, they had better go themselves. Two people couldn't be making it up. When they reached the big front piazza, there was no one on it and no one in the big sitting room. There was only that fresh young man at the desk whom they had often avoided. They hated to, but they thought they ought to tell him. He spoke to them first, making one of his fresh remarks, but they let that go. It was unimportant. Edie went up to the desk counter.

"I think the Hotel is on fire," she said clearly and seriously.

"Ah g'wan widjer," the young man said, trying to be funny in Irish.

Susan stepped up beside her. "There's smoke coming out of the roof," she said, nodding to help her words.

"All on a summer's day," said the young man, grinning.

It was hard to know what to do next. They wanted to save the Hotel, but they couldn't do it alone, and how could they manage this terrible person? Edie remembered something Father had said to Madam. "Go to the top, my dear. If you want something, always go to the top."

"Could we see the manager?" she said, hoarse from having to be so quiet when all the time the Hotel was burning up.

"He's having his lunch," said the young man.

"I can see him," said Edie, looking into the inner office. "I can see his arm." She raised her voice. "Mr. Manager, listen. The Hotel is on fire."

The manager's arm came up to put something in his mouth.

"Are you having trouble, MacKenzie?" he said. "Call the police."

They thought it was just a false alarm to scare them, but they weren't sure, so they waited. The manager got up and came out wiping his mouth.

"This is a very poor joke, young ladies," he said, "and we could have you arrested for it." Then he saw who they were. "I thought I told you to stay out of here," he said with a sort of roar.

"All the time your hotel is burning up," said Edie.

The manager just stared at them furiously. "All right," Edie said, "we'll do it ourselves. Come on, Susan."

She led the way to the flower shop. "The Hotel's on fire," she said into it quietly. Susan took the other side. "The Hotel's on fire," she said to the jewelers and walked out. They told the nut shop and the candy shop. Their owners came to their doors and stared at them. They were going to the dining room to tell the waiters when Edie stopped and put her hands to her face.

"Oh," she said, "The Littles! They're on the fourth floor with Hood, and they'll be asleep."

They did not even look in the direction of the elevator but raced for the stairs.

"MacKenzie," they heard the manager say, "go after those two panic raisers and *catch* them."

They heard MacKenzie fumbling with the latch behind the desk and heard him jump three steps at a time behind them. But they had a good start.

At the third floor, they were almost dead, but you could smell smoke there. MacKenzie didn't even try. On the fourth floor landing you could see it, and they just twisted out of his grasp when he did see it. That got rid of Mac-Kenzie. He didn't give them another thought but vaulted down the half flight without touching a step. Edie and Susan had to recover for a minute. There was smoke but not much. The corridor doors were always left open so that the sea breeze could come in, and that kept blowing it away.

"You take one side and I'll take the other," said Edie. "Try every door and keep yelling."

After they had yelled, they had to listen for an answer. It slowed them up a good deal and made them anxious. Perhaps they should have tried opening doors, too. In Palm Sands perhaps they would not be locked. Naturally Hood had locked hers. They found this out at the very last door.

"Now, Miss Edith, go away," Hood said from behind it.

"The children are asleep, and you've no call to make such a racket."

"Just open the door," said Edie. "Just open the door for a second."

Hood wouldn't. She was washing her hair, she said. Edie knew what that meant. She had taken off her switch and didn't want to be seen.

"Hood," said Edie, trying to sound reasonable. "The Hotel is on fire."

"None of your tricks now," said Hood. "I won't have them." She was retreating again to the bathroom—they could hear her voice go—and the smoke was getting a little thicker. If she could get The Littles out, Edie thought, she wouldn't care if Hood burned to a cinder. It would serve her right. But she couldn't leave Madam's children.

"Come on, Sue, we have to," she said.

They howled at the tops of their lungs and they hammered on the door with their fists and finally with their feet, and they kept it up until they heard Chris and Lou begin howling, too. At last Hood unlocked the door and opened it a crack. The smoke was right there, and a bit of it wisped right up to her nose.

"Holy Mother of God!" she said.

When Hood had to *do* anything, there was nobody like her. It was sentiments that got her mixed up. Now she did not wait a second, not even to pin up her hair or get her switch, not even to dress The Littles; she got them up in their pants and bare skins and had them at the door even before she had stopped their howling.

"Stop it, now," she said to them firmly. "It's only your

sister's fooling. Can we get them out, Miss?" she said to
Edie.

"Easy," said Edie. "Look, the back stairs are right
there."

The back stairs were outside. They had broad treads
and a rail, but they were high and long. Hood looked to
the other end of the corridor and saw that it was where
the smoke was coming from.

"All right, Miss," she said. She took the children's hands
and hurried toward the open door through which you
could see only sea and sky. She was just as afraid of
heights as Jane, but she was going as fast as she could
trudge. Good old Hood!

And now they were free! They turned to rush in the
direction of the smoke.

"Wait!" said Susan. "We might as well get their things."

They rolled the children's clothes in a ball and carefully
put Hood's switch in the middle. Then they threw it out
the window.

"I know something," said Edie.

She snatched washrags off the bathroom rack, doused
them with water, and gave one to Susan.

"The smoke," she said. "Father said to."

Then they raced—really free—for the center stairs.

There had not been anyone in the Hotel, not a soul. The
doors they had knocked at had given no answer. After the
fire was over, people could not stop talking about it. Susan
and Edie had to say over and over that there was nobody
around. Now they met them coming up the grand staircase. Some of them kept on going up in spite of the smoke,
but Edie and Susan preferred to get to the third floor even

though they had washrags. So far there was only the smell there and more and more people. They did what the others were doing. Most of the doors were open now, and the sights were perfectly glorious. Clothes, furs, evening wraps, laces, and every other kind of thing were being dumped into sheets spread out on the floors. Like the rest, they scrambled in bureau drawers, gathered up armsful, and added to the piles of the sheets. Men tied the sheets up and put them out the windows. Men down below tried to catch them, but they weren't very successful. When the sheets hit the ground, some of them burst open.

"There go Mrs. Vanderbilt's best clothes," said Susan as she saw one explode.

"Did you ever have so much fun in your life?" said Edie.

"Oh, but the poor Hotel," said Susan.

It was time to go down to the next floor. The smoke was beginning to come in large puffs. This time they used the outside stairs. Their washrags had gone out the window with Mrs. Vanderbilt's best clothes.

Everything on the next two floors was going out the windows. No one tried to fill sheets. Someone came down the corridor to say the fire had got to the Ladies Lounge. This created a kind of frenzy. The Ladies Lounge was in the exact center of the Hotel. It meant there was not much time left. The fire had begun to be so big that everything, somebody said, was simply melting in front of it. For the first time Edie realized that the Hotel—their Hotel—was really going to burn down. She and Susan couldn't save it. Although more and more men came to throw things out the windows, they couldn't save it.

Nobody could. She didn't know why, but tears began

running out of her eyes, and she became furious with the men who were working. They were having too good a time. They were laughing and making jokes about the belongings they were throwing out. Accidentally on purpose, she gave one of them a good kick on the shins, but with sneakers on you couldn't do much. All he said was:

"Hey, kid, look where you're going."

She began to feel sorry for the people whose things were all mixed up and getting dirty. How would they ever find them? Even if they could, all those beautiful things would be a mess.

One thing she saved herself. It was too little for anyone to notice—a bright blue stone on someone's bureau, about as big as a five cent piece, oval, and strangely carved. She put it in her pocket, and when she found some handkerchiefs in a drawer, she crammed one down on top of it. Nobody seemed to want it, and if it went out the window, it would be lost. She would keep it for a lucky stone. Right away it seemed to comfort her for the awful thing that was happening.

Finally even the first floor began to get hot, and the smoke was coming in billows. They could hear the fire roaring behind them. A man's voice began shouting.

"All out, all out."

He came down the corridor shooing people in front of him. When a helper would not leave, he caught his arm and swung him out of a room and toward the door. "OUT!" he said. It sounded like something Edie and Susan had heard before, so they looked at him. It was the manager.

"He gave us the evil eye. Did you see that?" said Susan as they ran.

"What do we care about him any more," said Edie. She was almost choking with smoke and tears. "Didn't he let the Hotel burn up!"

Out on the lawn they stood with the rest of the crowd to watch the Hotel go up in one stupendous, roaring volcano of fire. At almost the last minute, they saw a sight that made them hurriedly wipe off their smear of tears and almost laugh. Someone had found a baby somewhere, and he was at a first floor window with it. He tried to get out the window carrying it, but he didn't seem used to babies, and first he hit its head on the sash and then on the side as he tried to put his leg over. A little smoke was coming out past him, but the crowd did nothing. It all looked so easy. The ground was right there and the window was big. He did not try again. The baby was howling and throwing itself around, and he was having a time holding onto it. Discouraged, he held it out by its middle for someone to take. No one moved. The crowd thought the joke was on him. Just as Susan finally took a step forward, a man went past her and up to the window. The baby was delivered to him. And who had been holding it? Theodore!

Oh, glorious, glorious day!

The train had come in without a soul to meet it, and the whole family was there to watch him holding a squirming, howling baby. Edie was sure that her lucky stone had done this miracle. Palm Sands and even all of Florida by themselves could not have accomplished anything so really great.

Six

※

MADAM

There was no way to know that spring was coming in Palm Sands—unless Mr. Barlow pointed out little bright green things that suddenly came to life in crevices—except by the fact that instead of Edie being discussed, it was Madam and how she was to get back to Summerton without an attack of asthma. She was better; she was almost well. Edie wondered whether the lucky stone had had something to do with it. But the family, when they came for Easter, wondered if it was the new doctor, who was not at all interested in Madam's bronchial tubes but only in what he called "nerve strain."

He interviewed Father, and Father felt that Madam had for once found a doctor who showed some sense. Still, it didn't solve her getting from Palm Sands to Summerton. Father did not want her to go alone, and Hubert summed up what it might be like to travel with a dog, a bird, two small children, sixteen pieces of luggage, and an obstinate old nurse like Hood.

"That's nerve strain if you like," he said. He had once

made a similar trip, and he felt it would last him a life-
time.

For a very short time it looked as if Edie and Susan,
who had both miraculously been allowed to stay on in
Florida, might be chosen as her protectors. When Madam
had gone up to rest after lunch and everyone was congre-
gated on the porch to talk things over, it seemed as if four
pairs of eyes began looking at them.

"Why are we so interesting all of a sudden?" Edie said.

They had probably been talking about her behind her
back.

Father took out his cigar.

"Don't you think that you and Susan could come back
with your stepmother and manage to make her comfortable?" he said.

"Alone?"

Father nodded.

When Father nodded like that, not only in command
but also as if he wanted you to, it was almost impossible
not to nod back. Just the same she couldn't do it. What
did she and Susan know about taking care of a grown
person? Every time Father had left to go north, he had
said: "Take good care of your stepmother," and Edie had
answered: "I will." But they hadn't given it a thought,
except for not letting her know the things that would
worry her. All winter they had been perfectly willing to
do her errands, like finding her atomizer, her gloves, her
glasses, and her handkerchiefs, and carrying packages at
that new store she loved so well called "The Piggly-
Wiggly," or taking Jippy to walk once in a while, and this
was all Madam ever seemed to want. They went to the
beach with her to see she didn't drown. She wore so many

clothes when she bathed that it seemed only too likely. Otherwise, she was able to manage her life in Palm Sands perfectly well. But what in the world you could do with a grown person—if there were trouble—who didn't do what you told them, she couldn't imagine. Susan was not very helpful either.

"Suppose we got her on the train and she started dying," she said.

It was a terrible thing to stand out against Father, and some terrible things were said to her, but Edie kept on doing it right up to the time he left and even after he had said, with a sigh: "I wish I could do it myself." But he couldn't. In order for them to enjoy places like Palm Sands, he said, he had to tend to his job.

"Why not Jane?" said Edie in desperation.

Had she forgotten Jane had a job? She *had* forgotten it because although Jane was foolish sometimes, she couldn't have thought she would be so foolish as to get shut up in an office all day. She thought Jane might take a week off. But no, Father said Jane had to have a chance to make good.

"Well, I won't do it," said Edie, her back against the wall. "I'll run away."

It made Father sigh again. "I suppose I shall have to try to get a companion," he said.

His greatest difficulty was to try to explain it to Madam, who did not want a companion and thought that she would be beautifully taken care of on Cousin Lyman's train. "Besides, I'll have the girls," she said. Father groaned and did not even try to explain about them. He got her to give in by saying he would not have a moment's peace if he didn't know she was in good hands. "Let her

come for a week before you leave," he said, "so you can
get used to each other, and then I'll meet you in New York
and she can go about her business."

Edie and Susan thought this was a fine arrangement,
although Susan had to feel guilty. "Your stepmother has
been awfully nice to me," she said.

"One grownup ought to look after another," Edie said,
not guilty in the least.

Just the same, she agreed that they should keep track of
Madam until the companion came. They examined her at
mealtimes, and they thought they saw good signs. Her
eyes were as big as ever, she still picked at her food, there
was a sort of memory of panting around her, but every so
often she would sit back and draw long breaths and smile
a little to herself. It was different from what Edie could
remember for quite a while, so they thought it safe to stay
outside Spray Cottage if they stayed near enough for an
emergency. They spent a few days digging for crabs in the
sandy patch of lawn, and then Susan was sure God rewarded them for their thoughtfulness. Mr. Barlow came
back again, and this time instead of snakes or bones he
brought Mrs. Barlow. She was almost as big as her hus-
band, and she and Mrs. Cares seemed to be "best friends."
They talked and sewed and knitted and talked and walked
and played cards and talked. What better thing could
have happened? Edie and Susan rejoiced at first by running down the beach as far as they could from Spray
Cottage and flinging themselves into the water, and then
each day or night going to say good-by to their paradises.
They managed to visit the spider monkey, and Susan
kissed him. They were able to take one short nervous
swim in the black pool in sight of the flamingos, and they

pumped themselves exhausted around the marble paths
of the Marble Palace. They could not say good-by to the
Hotel because it wasn't there. It made them feel bad.

"We ought to be able to do *some*thing for it," Susan
said.

Its poor ashes lying there abandoned, with a poor little
black safe sticking up in the middle, made her ache, she
said. She and Edie hated the people who came to look at
the remains, and the Hotel people who did nothing about
disposing of them. Edie thought it would be a good thing
if the sea came in and washed them away. "Maybe a hurricane or a tidal wave," she said.

"It would wash us, too," said Susan. "I don't believe
they have 'em this time of year. I don't believe your stepmother would be here if they did."

It was she who thought that they could help the Hotel
out of its undignified situation by giving it a funeral. At
first Edie thought this was silly. To have a funeral, you
had to have a corpse.

"In India they burn corpses," said Susan. "My father
told me so. They scatter their ashes on rivers, and the
corpse gets eternal life. I don't quite see how," she added,
"but we could give the Hotel its chance, and it's a corpse
already."

She did not mean that they had to gather up *all* the
Hotel ashes. She did not even mean they were bound to
take them out to sea, but she felt it would be very comforting if they found a nice box and filled it with ashes,
buried it, and marked the grave.

It took quite a few days to do things properly. The box,
the very box they wanted, which had come from the
Hotel candy shop itself, still had barley sugar in it. They

took it out of the cupboard after every meal and offered it around, until finally Mrs. Barlow had taken the last piece. This box was worthy. It was big, the inside was metal, and the outside had lace paper. "A really good coffin," Susan said. They scraped the ashes hurriedly into their box at three o'clock one afternoon, that hour when everyone disappeared. It seemed to them, when they remembered, very appropriate. "Just when the Hotel burned down," said Edie.

They waited until dark to bury it. Then they scratched a deep hole in the depths of the shrubs and sea grass above the beach and, after the grave had been marked by stones, covered it with hibiscus blossoms. They had done a good job, they felt. It ought to have been enough. The Hotel ought to be pleased and satisfied. But as they stood looking at it, they were still unsure that it *was* enough for what they had felt about the Hotel.

"Maybe we ought to sing 'My Old Kentucky Home,'" said Susan.

They knew all the verses on account of having been to Miss Lincoln's together, and they sang them all. Edie's voice, very low and clear, carried across the surrounding sea grass into the darkness.

"That ought to do it," said Susan.

Edie agreed. Maybe the grasses would keep on singing and the Hotel would hear their sorrow forever. It was just what they had wanted.

In the meantime, they found, Mr. and Mrs. Barlow had been the perfect guardians for Madam. They had arranged for The Littles and Hood to take the train; they had seen them off; they had interviewed Madam's cook and persuaded her to stay an extra week. They had taken the car themselves to use in Cuba and Mrs. Barlow from now on would have to find out where Mr. Barlow left it, and the Barlows themselves were departing at just the right time. Madam's companion was coming tomorrow. There was hardly a moment when Edie and Susan would have to be on guard again. Even this moment was delightful. In it they realized that Spray Cottage was quiet again, the afternoon breeze was there, the palm trees were making the sound of rain, the sun and sand were hotter, and the smell of wood smoke and flowers was not interfered with by cigars. They would have a whole week of it while Madam's companion did her odd jobs and saw that she had no nervous strain. God and the lucky stone were still working for them.

They did not go with Madam to meet her companion. Mr. Barlow had advised against it. "Let them get acquainted before you two burst upon the scene," he had said.

They watched Madam get ready, put hatpins in her large white hat, gather up her gloves and parasol, and saw her go off down the path around the golf course. This was the moment they had meant to set off themselves for a ride down the County Road to see how far they could get, but they stood undecided. Just as she was about to start, Madam had turned to them and said: "Don't you two go away and leave me with this Mrs. Tilliams-Williams or whatever her name is."

"Well then, I guess we can't," said Susan as soon as Mrs. Cares could not hear.

It was a terrible moment. How could they do two exactly opposite things that two grownups had commanded?

Edie was in favor of Mr. Barlow. "If he's a professor, he ought to know what he's talking about."

Susan was in favor of Mrs. Cares. "It's an awful strain to be deserted," she said. She sat down on the front steps in her most obstinate manner, and Edie was obliged to leave her.

She was still there when Edie came back after quite a long while. She was not even consoling herself with gum or a book, just sitting with her chin in her hands. But Edie was not going to be sympathetic. She had gone for miles down the County Road and had seen an airplane, but it hadn't been any fun.

"Well, what's she like?" she said.

Susan put her head on one side and squinted one eye at her. "I don't believe your stepmother thinks she's quite a lady," she said.

"But what's she *like?*"

"She's small and she scuttles."

Mrs. "Tilliams-Williams" did not come to dinner. A tray was sent up to her. She was recovering from the trip, Madam said. Mrs. Cares did not come to breakfast; Mrs. Williams said she was resting. So much resting for grown-ups was not unusual, as the girls both knew, and they thought they noticed lots more good signs. Mrs. Williams was clean. She was the cleanest woman they could ever remember seeing. That ought to please Madam. Another thing was—she did not talk. That ought to please anybody. People who were not ladies, Edie asked Susan to remember, talked all the time. She hardly ate anything. After Mr. Barlow, that was wonderful. Cook would think so and so would the parlormaid. Her hair had no wisps in the back; she did not stick out her little finger from her coffee cup.

But she was small, and she did scuttle.

"I expect your grandfather would say that ladies have a more leisurely tread," said Susan, looking after her as she left the dining room.

"D'you think we ought to tell her?"

Susan could only shrug. "If you tell a grown person anything like that," she said, "they get mad. Even if you're trying to save their lives," she added mournfully.

The mournfulness, Edie knew, was because Susan felt Mrs. Williams' life might need to be saved unless she could be given the right information. But perhaps it wouldn't have done any good. By the end of the week there were about a thousand things Mrs. Williams, in spite of the first good signs, would have had to be told about. She shouldn't scuttle just a step behind Madam when they were walking, she shouldn't scuttle after her with glasses of milk, she shouldn't scuttle here and there like a beagle after what Madam had lost, and she should scuttle away when Madam's friends came. She didn't, though; she scuttled them in from the front door and into chairs and made scuttling remarks like: "Is this right, Mrs. Cares?" "Do you want this chair or that, Mrs. Cares?" Susan and Edie tried hints. They were very tactful. As they sat together in the swing hammock after lunch when Madam had gone upstairs, they talked with Mrs. Williams about Madam's friend, Mrs. Foster, as they watched her go away down the beach path.

"What I like is, she goes away when she's supposed to," Edie said.

"And she takes such lovely long steps," said Susan.

Mrs. Tilliams-Williams didn't catch on.

"Mrs. Foster is a lovely woman," she said, "very lovely." But she thought her mannish. "Not at all becoming in a woman," she said. She was sitting in a rocking chair, and she made it rock so it grunted.

"It's better than being kittenish," said Edie.

This was so plain that she had to fix her eyes on the sea.

But honestly, Mrs. Tilliams-Williams might as well have been deaf.

"Wouldn't you think she'd think I'd know about my own stepmother?" Edie said.

"I don't believe you can expect grownups to have that much sense," Susan said.

Anyway, Mrs. Williams did exactly the same things as before, and so did Madam. Madam looked at her both over her glasses and then again after she took them off.

The day Mrs. Williams stepped backwards onto Jippy when Madam waved away a glass of milk, Mrs. Williams had to go to her room and pull down the shades. She could not stand being looked at so much, and probably she could not stand Jippy who went around ki-yiing with one paw in the air.

The day before they were to leave Palm Sands, practically everything in Spray Cottage disappeared—the trunks, the cook, the parlormaid, and Mrs. Tilliams-Williams. The girls had expected the other things to go. Madam had told them they were to eat the last day at Mrs. Foster's and do their own picking up, but Mrs. Williams was supposed to stay to take care of Madam on the train to keep her from having any nervous strain. She had not come out of her room or pulled up the shades since stepping on Jippy. She had not answered when Edie was sent up to tell her not to be an idiot, but they knew she was there because she let in her meals. Then all of a sudden her door was opened and she was not inside. They could not help wondering if she had been murdered. In the newspapers, if someone disappeared suddenly, it almost always turned out to be murder.

"Not by your stepmother, I do hope," said Susan.

It made Edie uneasy. Almost anyone would like to have done it, and Jippy was still going around holding up his paw.

"Even if she did do it, how could she get rid of the body?" Edie said.

"Maybe Mr. Barlow helped," said Susan.

"You're the most ghoulish person I ever heard of," Edie said. "If you don't stop thinking up things, I'll turn the Lucky Stone on you."

"I'm protected by God," said Susan tauntingly.

They were quarreling because they were both upset. The companion had vanished just when her real duties were to begin, and they both had the same thought. If anything was likely to bring on an attack of asthma, it would certainly be a thing like murder. In spite of being angry with each other, they hung around Mrs. Cares to observe her breathing until she had to say, "You *are* under my feet, this morning. What's the matter?"

"Did you notice Mrs. Williams isn't here?" said Edie.

"I managed to get rid of her," Madam said, and this time she looked at Edie over her glasses.

After that Susan was terrible. Later she said it was because she had been scared into fits. She asked Edie if she remembered the Ten Commandments. She said: "What about the police?" She also said that the Cares family were known to do some queer things, but she had never thought they would murder anybody. Edie had to leave her. She could think up ghoulish things by herself if she wanted, but Edie was not going to listen to any more of them. If Madam had gotten Mr. Barlow to push Mrs. Williams off the pier or something, she herself would have to kill Susan if she started to say a word about it, but she did not like having to think of this. She walked to the Indians in the village and bought an alligator for fifty cents and then went to the Piggly-Wiggly for raw meat.

Not a thing happened. God did not appear holding the Ten Commandments, the police did not come, Madam did not get an attack of asthma, and they had wonderful meals at Mrs. Foster's. No one seemed to care a bit about Mrs. Tilliams-Williams. Just the same, every single thing in the world was spoiled because Edie and Susan could not possibly speak to each other. This was because Susan would not give in. Edie asked her over and over a hundred thousand times. "Would you tell?" Susan answered the same every time. "I'd have to."

"I thought you liked my stepmother," Edie kept saying, "and wanted to take care of her because she had been nice to you."

She could see that that made Susan squirm a bit.

"You can't like murderesses," said Susan inside her lips.

They couldn't speak even after they got on the train and found they had a compartment to themselves again and could have the two dogs with them this time. They could only speak about this one thing. They watched Widgy and Jippy having a wonderful time looking at the sights at all the stations, but they themselves were glum. They did not even want to play parchesi. Once an hour they went to the other end of the car where Madam had her own compartment and observed how she was breathing. Although she spent part of the morning in bed in her pink ribboned bed jacket, she looked as comfortable as anything.

"Would you tell?" Edie said one last time.

"I'd have to," said Susan.

"You have to admit she doesn't look like a murderess," said Edie.

Susan only put her lips together and wouldn't answer at all. She finally put her feet up and went to sleep on the pillow the porter had given her. She could do that when the most important question in the world was still undecided! Edie looked steadily out the window, hating her and everything, hating and hating and hating, and mostly she hated that Tilliams-Williams for getting herself murdered. Whatever Mr. Barlow had said, Florida was the dullest-looking place she ever saw. There was nothing in it, but nothing, and she hated Florida, too. It didn't even interest her when a train on another track caught up with them and went past, going like the dickens. It didn't interest her that it slowed down and Cousin Lyman's train caught up with it. It did this lots of times until the trains seemed to be having a race. She woke up a little, enough to hope that Cousin Lyman's train would win. When Cousin Lyman's dropped behind, she was sorry. Then it caught up again, and both trains slowed down, but not much, so that Edie without meaning to found herself pushing Cousin Lyman's along. It gave her a chance to hate the people in the other train, especially a lot of dirty-

faced children pressing their noses against the windows.
They all seemed to have colds. Why couldn't their mothers wipe their noses? The other train was slowing, and
Cousin Lyman's surged forward. Glory be, his was going
to win! The children were being left behind, and Edie
watched carefully to see what faces would come next.
Suddenly she had to press her own face against the glass.
What was she seeing? Her eyes couldn't believe it. She
gave Susan a tremendous whack.

"Sue, look! Get up. *Look!* Hurry, oh, *hurry.* Who's
that? Quick!"

Susan, the lump, took her time.

"I'll kill you!" she said.

"Never mind now," said Edie, collapsing. "It's too late.
Oh, you lump," she said. "Oh, you terrible LUMP."

But it wasn't too late. Cousin Lyman's train was slowing down again. Edie got on her feet. "Watch!" she said.
"Just watch carefully; that's all I ask you to do."

The other train drew up a little, and both ran level for a
minute. "NOW!" said Edie. "LOOK!"

"Oh, my," said Susan in a whisper, and sat down suddenly. "Oh, my heavenly MY. Do you think it's her ghost?"

"I'll show you!" said Edie. She collected the two dogs
in her arms and put them at the window. She made them
jump and bark, and herself waved and shouted and
knocked. Of course, Mrs. Tilliams-Williams could not
hear, but the excitement somehow made her look up, and
there was her full face as clear as daylight. She even
frowned at them, shook her head, and turned away. It
only lasted a minute. Cousin Lyman's train put on speed,
and Tilliams-Williams was left behind for good. They
waited and waited to get another look—Susan's obstinacy

would not give in. How did she know, she said, that Tilliams-Williams's ghost wouldn't return from the grave.

"She wasn't even buried," said Edie. But she saw that
she was getting off the track. "Come on. Let's go see my
stepmother," she said, "and we'll find out."

They did not find out, however, until they got to the
Pennsylvania Station in New York. Madam, who was doing a jigsaw puzzle on a board on her lap, asked them to
come in and help, but she would not discuss anything. "I
could not stand Tilliams-Williams," she said. "Don't even
mention her. It affects my breathing."

At the Pennsylvania Station they were asked to find
Father as quickly as they could, and taking a look at
Madam who was clutching her handbag and sitting very
upright taking quick breaths, they did find him and
brought him to the right end of the car. They were just in
time.

"Where's your companion, my dear?" Father said when
Madam had been handed out.

"I'm here, Mr. Cares," a voice said over his shoulder.
"And you shall pay for the way I've been treated. Indeed
you shall."

And there stood Mrs. Tilliams-Williams almost vibrat-
ing with indignation, all her scuttliness turned into rage.

But, as Edie said to Susan later, what could poor old
Tilliams do with Madam looking at her as if she were a
scolding sparrow. Mr. Barlow had turned out to be a real
kidnaper and had "very gently," as Mrs. Cares said, put
her on the wrong train. "Who could help that?"

"I *suspect* your stepmother," said Susan. "But as long as
she isn't a murderess, 'Judge not that ye be not judged.'"

"You'd have told, I suppose?"

"I'd have had to," said Susan.

For days and days after she got home, Edie could not go to see anyone that obstinate.

Spring was always wonderful in Summerton, but this year Edie thought she had never seen anything like it. The relations seemed to have arranged for blossoms to pile on blossoms or, if not that, to have them shoving each other out of the way so there would be room for more. Aunt Charlotte had a little hill outside her garden wall that was capped by daffodils, Uncle Warren's brook was bordered with violets, and all the family dairy farms were spread, dotted, and patched by apple blossoms, some of them white, but some like strawberry ice cream. Everyone had lilacs somewhere, and Uncle Charles's peonies got to be fat pink sofa cushions. Widgy, she thought, ought to see it all. When she went to bed, she arranged his bed by the window so that he could enjoy the night smell, sometimes of lilacs and sometimes a combination of things so wonderful that she didn't know herself where it could come from—could it really be the sea from so far away? Anyway, it made her think of swimming, boats, and hot piazza boards combined with rose vines and cut grass. She and Susan now had school on the Stoninghams' screened porch, where, at any minute, they could be distracted by what went across the lawn. Mr. Gibbs himself seemed a good deal distracted. He read to them from really good books like *The Wizard of Oz* and *Beautiful Joe* instead of *David Copperfield* and *Vanity Fair*. Mrs. Stoningham brought out first hot cross buns at recess and then, as it got warmer, vanilla ice cream with mashed strawberries. The ponies were as fat as butter and needed exercise. In

the afternoons, instead of hunting for colored leaves, as
they had done in the autumn, they tried to see how many
different kinds of green there were in the Summerton
countryside. The cows began being let out, and they stood
up to their knees in thick grass.

"How *I* would like to be eating it," Edie said to Susan.

Perhaps that was the best sight of all. And as soon as
they had found the best sight, they found one still better.
For instance, the three weeny frogs that sat on the edge of
Aunt Isabelle's fountain looking at her forget-me-nots.
They could hardly keep from taking one apiece home to
live with them forever.

Madam was so well that she took trips with Father.
Theodore was in training for the crew at Harvard College,
so that he had to be very careful of himself and could not
come home and eat brown bread with cream or Yorkshire
pudding with gravy, and Hubert, when he came, brought
boys who, even if they were rather snobbish and did not
much want girls around, were quite a pleasure to look at.
Over weekends when the girls were alone, Susan was allowed to stay at the Lawn House, and Miss Lincoln was
imported from the village.

"But who minds her," Edie said.

She let them do everything they wanted except eat
French-fried potatoes. She said these were indigestible.

"Our families let us eat them," the girls said together.

That made Miss Lincoln burst into tears. They gave up
trying to have French-fried potatoes and made Miss Lincoln play croquet for hours on end instead.

"Oh, the spring, the spring, the spring," they chanted
while out riding.

The Reservoir basins were as blue as Madam's sapphire

ring, and little blue irises fringed them at the bottom of
the relations' lawns.

It rained on some days, but who cared when the birds
had such a good time. Edie would walk over to Susan's
across the swamp in order to see how good she still was at
walking the tufts, and they would give the rabbits a treat
by letting them hop around the Stoninghams' living room.

There was only one trouble with the spring. Edie had
lost her lucky stone. When she changed her dress one
morning, she had taken it out of her pocket and laid it on
her bureau. It was just the moment when Chris had come
in to hop around and ask questions. Chris didn't steal it;
she just took it and put it in her own pocket so that she
could show it to her mother. And she did show it to her
mother and then had to come back and tell Edie that
Madam wanted to see her.

Madam had had the lucky stone on the blanket beside
her, and Edie went to pick it up. "I didn't even know it
was gone," she said. "Thanks a lot."

"Is it yours?" her stepmother had said.

"I've had it quite a long time. Nobody wanted it," said
Edie. "It's my lucky stone. It does things for me. Really!"
she added, looking at her stepmother's face.

"It's been advertised for," Madam said, "for quite a long
time. Ever since the fire."

"It has! Who by?"

It turned out to be some old professor, and the lucky
stone was a scarab that had come out of a tomb. No wonder it had done things for her! But the old professor
wanted it back so badly that he had put things in the
paper about it. He had even made them sift the hotel
ashes.

"It would have been burned up if I hadn't rescued it," said Edie. "It would have been charred to bits. What did he leave it around for?"

Nothing she could say made Madam see that the lucky stone was really hers, not even when she showed her that it was probably the stone that had gotten rid of Mrs. Tilliams-Williams so easily.

She had to lose the lucky stone, and it was a very bad time to lose it. Grandfather had come back from the city, and she was having to go to church with him again. She had depended on the stone to help her about Greg Robinson. Susan, of course, was delighted.

"Now that you've lost that old idol," she said, "you'll *have* to depend on God. And you better hurry up. He could be mad at you, you know, the way He was with Aaron."

That wouldn't have scared her, but Greg Robinson was in the sixth form now and he was the baseball captain besides, and besides that he was better looking than ever, and if she didn't get him to look at her before his graduation the twelfth of June, there would be no hope forever. If she had had the lucky stone to take to church, she believed it would have done it, but it had had to go back to the old professor. She didn't care at all that she had gotten a thank-you letter from him, enclosing a five dollar bill. Five dollars was a large fortune, as Susan had said, but she had put it in the plate at church, she was so mad at the professor.

"It might do you some good," said Susan, "except that God can see your insides."

To make up for this, she suggested that Edie begin to

learn a little more religion. "If you do it in earnest," she said, "it might get you somewhere."

After two Sundays when Edie could not even see Greg Robinson's face in the choir from where she sat with Grandfather, and the red-headed boy in front of him had put out his tongue at her because she was staring—when he was kneeling down, too!—she was willing to do whatever Susan said.

"All right, you'd better learn the catechism," said Susan.

They left Susan's rabbits, they shut Widgy up, and they took a prayer book to one of the bathhouses beside the school swimming pool in order to be as private and earnest as possible, but from the very first they had trouble with giggling. It wasn't anything to giggle about, Edie knew that, and Susan was horrified at herself. They could keep straight faces getting past the N. and M., but when it came to Edie's keeping her hands from "picking and stealing," and Susan having to renounce "pomps and vanities," they found themselves tottering from the bathhouse holding their stomachs. "It means you'll have to cut off your beautiful braid," said Edie, the tears running down her face.

"It does not!"

"It does, it does!"

They tried skipping because there were so many words Susan couldn't explain, even when she didn't have to giggle, but then Susan came to the phrase, "My good child," and they were ruined again.

"I don't understand," said Susan crossly. "It can't mean you, no matter how many catechisms you learn."

"It does, it does," said Edie again.

They had to give it up because Susan was sure they were being sacrilegious.

"You're not supposed to laugh at prayer books," she said.

"Well, I didn't mean to," said Edie, "but I didn't know they were so funny."

Susan thought that even more sacrilegious and went home in a huff. She said she would not let Edie come to her house again until she had repented. If Edie wanted to go to hell, she could go, but she wasn't going with her.

"Maybe you better," Edie said, and added, as she had said before, "There won't be any rabbits in heaven; they make too much of a mess."

Susan stalked off with her prayer book and did not even look back, so Edie stalked home, too. She bet she had given Susan a pinch with that last sentence, and she was glad of it. Susan was always thinking everybody was going to hell but herself.

Still, Edie did not seem to be able to get what she wanted by herself. Greg Robinson not only did not look at her in church on Sunday, but he also wasn't in the choir. He was not even there. She had a most awful feeling of fright. Perhaps he was sick, and she would never see him again in all her life. Quite a homely boy carried the cross instead, and she hoped he would break his leg or something. He had no right to be doing it.

Two days later she went to the bottom of the Stoninghams' lawn, stood on the wall, and yelled for Susan. She did not like doing it because she was sure she could be heard for miles around. It was the first of June, and school was over for her and Susan, but Hubert's school was still going and boys wandered out and around.

She had to yell three times, and when Susan did come out, she was disagreeable. "Don't you come up here," she said.

Edie could not yell a whole explanation. She had to shorten it up. "I've learned the 19th Psalm," she screamed. "All of it," she added when Susan looked like hesitating. "I've repented." She took a few steps nearer. "Want to hear it?"

They did not risk any more catechism or anything that was in the prayer book, but Edie had learned the longest psalm in the Bible and five verses of a hymn, because Susan was sure that it would show a spirit of what she called self-sacrifice.

"What's that?" said Edie.

"Doing things for others, you goof."

"I'm doing this for myself."

"Well," said Susan, "if you are, I don't think you'll get much out of it."

She did, though. At least she did at first. The next Sunday she had such a good feeling about who was coming up the aisle that she turned around to look just as the choir reached their pew, and she looked right into the eyes of Greg Robinson. They were as blue as the sea at Palm Sands at late evening. She didn't know why she didn't fall flat on her face, seeing something so beautiful, and when it was time to pray, she flopped onto her hassock so that it squeaked, glad to be in the private dark of her hands. Well, so Susan was right about God after all. Even the Lucky Stone could not have arranged things so neatly and wonderfully, not so that she would have turned her head at just the right second, not so that Greg Robinson would have moved his eyes for once in her di-

rection. So now she would have to be good for the rest of
her life. But that wasn't going to be hard. She felt like
being good. She felt like beginning right away. When the
sermon began, she did not as usual try to see Greg Robinson sitting on the other side of the red-headed boy. She
did not even look at the red-headed boy to see if he would
make faces as usual. She meant to be really good. Instead,
she picked up a hymn book in order to learn a hymn of
thankfulness. She opened it with great care so that neither
Grandfather nor the clergyman would notice and began at
the first page to see if she could find an appropriate one.
On the third page she was distracted by some writing.
"Turn to page 32," it said. This was exciting! There was a
message for someone, and she had come across it. On page
32 it said: "Turn to page 67." At page 67 she looked up
hard at the pulpit to show the clergyman she was paying
attention, but she had seen that it said: "Turn to page
103." Her hands turned pages while she still kept her face
raised, but she took a quick glance when she thought she
had turned enough. One more page. "Turn to 142," it
said. Maybe it was a joke, maybe there would be nothing,
but she couldn't stop looking. The numbers took her to
the end of the hymnal. Blooey, there was nothing.
But on the very last page, which was blank and white,
was "Turn Over." Now there would be the message.
It would have to be there, or what was the point of all
those numbers? At least there would be a joke or something. There was something. It was a picture drawn in
pencil, a picture of a donkey sitting up like a begging dog
and the donkey was dressed in a French sailor's fishing
suit and had a beret over one ear. Underneath the picture
it said: "Who's a—?"

Edie closed the hymnal very, very quietly, put it in the rack, and looked up at the clergyman for a minute. Then she let her eyes slide down to the red-headed boy. It was he, of course. And there he was as plain as day, hardly able to keep a straight face. He had been watching through the whole thing. She was sure of that. Now he was leaning back, looking as pious as anything, with his hands folded in his lap. At that moment, Edie thought her heart stopped. She saw that Greg Robinson, behind the red-headed boy, had been watching, too, and now he looked quickly away, down at his prayer book, but his face got bright pink, his shoulders began to shake, and she could see that he was having a hard time keeping the laugh inside of him, keeping his mouth straight. She had to take her eyes away so that her heart would start beating again, and she did not look back. She pretended to be interested in Mr. Hazard, the clergyman, so interested that she couldn't move. She had to do it to give her time to collect the pieces of herself that seemed to have been blown in every direction. It was lucky it was a good long sermon or she would never have been able to get together enough to walk out of church properly beside Grandfather.

That Sunday couldn't have been a better June day—hot in the sun and cool in the shade—and Hubert thought he had arranged things so that he could enjoy it to the full. He had invited Phil Phillips and Custard Clark for Sunday dinner and had told them what to expect. Roast beef, fresh asparagus, and strawberry ice cream. All they could eat. His stepmother was quite a remarkable woman; they wouldn't mind her at all, he said. After dinner he had planned a game of one-old-cat on the terrace lawn, and he mentioned his young sister.

"She's a good kid, and what's more important, she can throw straight," he said.

He meant not only to enjoy himself but also to show off his family and give everyone a good time. After he had tactfully questioned his friends and found they did not object to kids if they knew how to behave, he contemplated letting Chris and Lou stand in the back field and pick up balls. But thinking it over, he decided to add: "Well, you can't always depend on Edie, but she's got lots of sex appeal, so most people don't mind much what she does."

Phil and Custard had nodded understandingly. "Blazes," one of them said, "we'll get out of this prison."

"You're blamed right," said the other.

They were getting out the very next week for summer vacation, but it seemed as if the time would never come. Hubert felt fine to be their deliverer and thought he had done everything he could to make the occasion a success. They all walked over to the Lawn House together as soon as church was over, in clean shirts, wearing ties, and with lots of water on their hair. They had no idea that before they got to the Lawn House steps, somebody in the shrubbery would throw eggs at them and throw them straight.

"If that's what you call sex appeal!" Custard Clark said, trying to get the mess off with his bare hands.

Hubert said nothing. He laughed in a hollow way and led them to Gander and commanded her to do anything that would get off egg.

"Glory be!" Gander said. "Aren't you too old, Master Hubert, to be after having disputes with eggs?"

Hubert again had to laugh hollowly.

"Where's Edie?" he said.

"As if I would know the whereabouts of that one," said Gander.

Dinner was all that he had hoped. There were mountains of asparagus, and Madam served it on toast that was soaked with butter. Madam herself looked wonderful and couldn't have been more tactful, urging not only two helpings, but three on them all. Father did not try to talk about baseball but told them about a bridge he was building in Mississippi. It was as good an attempt to be interesting as Hubert could remember, and Phil and Custard seemed to like it. Anyway it covered up—or almost—the looks and behavior of Edie. She had put on her French boy's fishing suit, her hair was all tousled, and she sat through the entire meal staring, just staring, and not saying a word. Phil tried her out once, just once, because she answered in a loud voice: "You are nothing but a man. Shut up and leave me alone."

Phil turned very red and everyone looked at her, but she didn't mind that at all. She looked back as if she owned the earth. Why Father didn't send her upstairs, Hubert would never know. He almost wished Theodore was at home to settle her hash for her. But then, he might not have been able to catch her. Edie was very hard to catch once she knew you were after her. Like that afternoon. Or before lunch for that matter. Though all three of them had dashed for the shrubbery after the egg-throwing, there had been nobody there. And the afternoon was worse. Although, in spite of everything, Edie had been asked politely if she would like to play baseball, she had simply said: "Not with you nuts," and stalked off.

Just the same she would not let anyone else play. She somehow got Chris and Lou to turn into loons, and she directed the loons what to do from a safe place beyond the barberry hedge. At least it was safe until they made a concerted attack. Then they found she had tied up her pony to a gutter pipe at a corner of the house and was on him and galloping off with her stirrups swinging before they could get there. Custard almost had her once. He put out his hand to catch a stirrup leather but had reached too far and fallen flat on his face. Edie turned and watched while he brushed himself off and took the grass off his face and the dirt off his hands.

"Pickled pie-faced peanuts," she called. She had learned this from Chris, but it was much more insulting when she said it.

When they got back to the terrace lawn, the ball and the bat had disappeared, and so had Chris and Lou.

That devil Willy McHenry, Fatty's brother, who had only been asked to come to make another player, had gone home, but not without saying: "If you can't manage to keep a bunch of babies in order, I guess it's no use sticking around."

Hubert was not going to apologize to Willy McHenry. He had always been obnoxious, but he did say some apologetic things to his friends.

"Almost my entire family seems to have gone nuts," he said. "Maybe you better go on back and let me see if I can settle it."

It was the most completely ruinous time he could remember for a long while, and he had to sit with his arms around his knees for a long time in the middle of the terrace lawn trying to think what to do about it. If he could have gotten within shouting distance of Edie, he thought maybe he could have asked her what she thought she was doing. He could have said lots of things. Hadn't he always thought she was a good kid? Hadn't he always been on her side? What was she trying to spoil his Sunday for? Had she gotten mixed up and thought he was Ted? What had he ever done to her, anyway? Did she really have to be as awful as she looked this Sunday? He could try to appeal to her better nature, if she had any.

Hubert had been able to think of nothing that was any good by the time his stepmother came out. He couldn't have been gladder to see anyone. He got up and took a chair beside her.

"Honestly," he said, "oughtn't something to be done about that kid?"

"I suppose you mean Edie," Madam said.

"That I do," said Hubert. "The boys have gone home. They couldn't stand it. Frankly, I can't either. I shall have a nervous breakdown if I ever have to set eyes on her again in this life." He glanced sideways at his stepmother to see how she was taking it. Ted was convinced that Madam showed what he called "gross favoritism" for Edie.

Madam just looked out over the lawn with the fingers of one hand tight inside the fingers of the other. It was not "gross favoritism" this time, at any rate. She just didn't know what was the matter either. But Hubert was sure something had to be done.

"All of a sudden she's got this crazy, mad prejudice against men," he said. "Is she absolutely nuts?"

"You all tease her a good deal," Madam said, leaning forward and looking at her shoes.

"Is she going to be one of these man-haters?" he said. "Why not just shut her up for a while until she comes to? She's just running amuck, and that means crazy. You don't want her in an asylum, do you?"

Madam did not think Edie had come to that. She thought that perhaps Father could do something. Hubert was doubtful, but she thought he might try it. "Give him instructions then," he said. "Give him the right instructions. Tell him her whole future life is at stake."

After that, he went back to school himself. What more could he do?

When Edie could be found, which was long after Hubert had gone, she was told that Father wanted to see her in his office. Every Cares knew what that meant—Father, tipping back in his chair and saying he could no longer put up with you. She did not care in the least. She would tell him that she could no longer put up with him or anybody. Madam had taken her lucky stone, Susan was a hypocrite who didn't know anything, all the men in the world were devils, Chris and Lou were telltales, and "that old God was no good," so she went immediately to the office the minute Gander summoned her and stood in front of Father. Father was tipped back as usual, but he was not smoking, and his mustache was a little crooked. She thought he must be madder than he ever had been. She looked right at him, ready for anything.

"I don't think I can let you behave like this to your stepmother," Father said.

"She took my lucky stone," said Edie.

"It wasn't your lucky stone," Father said. "And you seem to have mixed it up with something else, God perhaps."

"That old God," said Edie. "He can't do a thing."

Father had to light a cigar after that. It took him a long time. He had to find the cigar, find the matches, and get it going. She kept herself together, ready for him, and did not even shift her feet. It was his turn again.

"Did it ever occur to you," Father said, after a lot of silent puffs, "that God might want an intelligent, strong, capable girl like you to do things on her own and not depend on charms or spells or magic or even on Him? It's just possible He may have a good deal to do."

"That old God," said Edie again, but she wasn't so sure this time.

"How is He to get it all done if the women don't help him? Those careless boys," Father said, "what good are they? They think of nothing but high-jinks. Think it over. There are a lot of people less able than you who may need attention—mostly men, I am very much afraid—and because you are an exceptionally bright and promising young lady, He may be depending on you." Father flicked his cigar.

"What for?"

"Why," said Father, considering his cigar ash, "to get along without rubbishy lucky stones and take care of yourself. Think it over."

Edie did not exactly stumble as she came out of the office, but she had to be careful how she placed her feet. She had a feeling as if they might run off with her somewhere—carry her up to the stars, jump her over the moon, try to swim the Atlantic Ocean. She made them walk sedately through the hall and out the front door, and by that time she knew where she was going. Father had said a lot of things that were good sense. He had said a lot of things that were the best things she had ever heard in her life, but there was one thing she would have to prove. She would have to do something to see if God would really take care, supposing she did not depend on magic or lucky stones. She would have to do something dangerous that she was scared of, that she might die from, and see once and for all whether He really did want her to get on by herself. She wouldn't ask Him a thing. She stood in the drive wondering what she could do. The Reservoir basin? The barn roof? Tree climbing? Jim McHale's savage dog? She suddenly thought of how much she had already done. As much as any boy she had ever heard of. And I'm only eleven years old, her mind said. But still she had to do this one more thing. Looking out to the meadows, she saw that the cows had been let into the new thick grass at the bottom of the hill. She looked harder. Whiz! They had let the bull out with them. It wasn't the biggest bull. He was never let out. He lived behind enormous bars, and no one was allowed near him. It was a pretty good bull, though, not just a bullock. All right, she would go down and walk past him in her red trousers, and she'd better hurry because she could almost feel her courage slipping down into her sneakers. The minute she was under the fence and standing in the tall grass, every cow raised its head, and the bull, too. They kept chewing for a minute and then stopped, giving her their full attention. The bull nosed the grass, then raised his head and bellowed, not loud, but he was paying attention, too, and was saying so. Edie did not stop, but her courage was in her sneakers all right. Only her feet would go on. Her real self was running as hard as it could go for the fence, sobbing with fright. She touched the first cow faces, and they backed away a little, leaving the bull a clear path. She let him look at her and saw that his little eyes were alarmed and alert. She took a step nearer. Slowly and slowly she went nearer still. He bellowed again and pawed the ground, but he did not move. Slowly she stretched out a hand. She would just give him the lightest, slightest touch, and that would be enough. He didn't seem interested in her red trousers, but only in her hand that was coming nearer and nearer. Just as it was above his nose, a long rough tongue came out of his mouth and licked it. It startled her so that she jumped back, and then the bull came forward. He wanted another lick. She took more steps backwards, her hand held out as if she would let him have it, and he came forward again. This was really terrible. She would have to walk backwards to the fence, and any minute he might decide to run at her. The cows, she could see, looked surprised and were watching to see what would happen. One of them, one beautiful, wonderful one of them, gave a low, soft moo. The bull liked it better than licking her hand and stopped. This was the minute! Now she could run. But, of course, in that thick, high grass nobody could run. She turned and, taking as high long steps as she could, went through the grass, with her back feeling like ice. Once she took a quick look over her shoulder. It seemed to be a mistake because it started the bull toward her, walking fast and then trotting a little. Then she did run, almost like a jack rabbit, and suddenly the fence was there and she was over it. She had to spend a few minutes on her stomach breathing hard into the grass. When she got up, the bull was right there puffing through the fence.

"Here," she said, "here," and held her hand through, first patting his hairy nose and then letting him lick.

"And thanks," she said, "thanks very much."

As she looked at him and his woolly face, she had another idea. He was such a nice bull. Why not take him up to the house and show him off? Slowly, carefully, she opened the gate and let him out and shut it again in the face of all those wondering cows. In fact, in the face of everybody.

She walked up the hill with the bull behind her. They were all there for some reason, the entire family—even Hubert, who had come back to see what there was for supper—staring at her from the grass circle.

"Oh, Edie, darling, for heaven's sake be careful!" cried Madam, in alarm.

"Edie, good Lord! Don't be a fool!" roared Father.

But Edie walked the bull right around the grass circle and said to Hubert as she went by, "I *did* it, I *did* it. Look, I *did* it!"

"What did you do?" said Hubert, backing away carefully. "Just another of your danged things."

"None of the rest of you ever dared do it. None of you *men*," she said. "I led a live bull around just the way I'd lead Widgy. And now I'll put him back."

Quietly and triumphantly she did put him back and returned smelling her hands. They were delicious.

That night when she got into bed, she felt very big and proud. But just at the last minute, before she fell asleep, a little thought wriggled into her mind. It's true that God had taken care of her. She was perfectly sure of that. She could depend on it; but all the same, it was an awfully, awfully nice bull.